THE GUNSMITH

#65

SHOWDOWN IN RIO MALO

The Gunsmith by J.R. Roberts

THE GUNSMITH

#65

SHOWDOWN IN RIO MALO

J.R. ROBERTS

SPEAKING VOLUMES, LLC
NAPLES, FLORIDA
2014

THE GUNSMITH
#65 SHOWDOWN IN RIO MALO

ISBN 978-1-61232-668-9

For more exciting
eBooks, Audiobooks and more visit us at
www.speakingvolumes.us

Chapter One

Clint Adams was sitting in the saloon called Rick's Place—the finest saloon in Labyrinth, Texas—with the owner, Rick Hartman, when a boy came in carrying a telegram, looking for him.

"Come here, Jimmy," Hartman said, calling the boy over. Jimmy looked to be about seven or eight years old, and he watched the Gunsmith with wide eyes.

"Hello, Mr. Hartman."

"What have you got, son?"

"I got a telegram for Mr. Gunsmith."

"How much?"

Jimmy's face took on a pensive look as he chewed his bottom lip.

"Two bits?"

"That's too much—" Hartman said, when Clint Adams interrupted him.

"It's okay, Rick. Cheap at the price. Here you go, Jimmy," Clint said, tossing the boy a quarter.

"Gee, thanks, Mr. Gunsmith."

"You can call me Clint, Jimmy."

"Really? Thanks! Wait till I tell Ma."

The boy went running happily from the saloon, and Clint unfolded his telegram.

"Now you did it," Rick said. "I'll have to let him call me Rick from now on."

"Is he a good friend of yours?" Clint asked Rick.

"He is, but not as good a friend as I'd like his mother to be."

"Oh, a new one? And a married one?" Clint asked, the telegram forgotten for a moment.

"Widowed. You know I don't go after married women, Clint."

"Is she attractive?"

"Very attractive."

"When do I get to meet her?"

Rick Hartman leaned forward, smiled, and said, "You don't. What does your telegram say?"

"Want to keep this one for yourself, huh? She must be special."

"Read your telegram."

"This is me," Clint said, straightening out the sheet of paper, "reading my telegram."

Clint read it while Rick Hartman leaned back and thought about Jimmy Kendrick's mother, Dorothy. She and her son had come to town less than a month ago, and Rick had immediately been attracted to her. He thought she felt the same way, but if she did, she was slow in saying so. That was okay though. He was willing to wait. This was a very different kind of woman than any other he'd ever been involved with before, and he was content to take it slow.

"Well, what do you know?" Clint said slowly.

"About what?" Rick asked. When he realized that Clint was referring to the telegram, he asked, "Good news?"

"Do you remember my mentioning Joe Bags?"

"Sure. He's a deputy somewhere now, ain't he?"

"He's been a deputy in quite a few places." It hadn't always been that way though. Bags might have been on his way to take a different path if he hadn't met Clint Adams1 and then met up with him again later.[2]

"Does he have a new job now?"

"He sure does, but not as a deputy. He says here he's been elected sheriff of Rio Malo, in New Mexico."

"I guess congratulations are in order. Why don't you wire him back?"

"I've got a better idea," Clint said, folding the telegram.

"Uh-oh."

"What?"

"You've got it again."

"Got what?"

Rick lowered his voice dramatically and said, "The wanderlust."

"I don't have it again," Clint corrected his friend, "I've got it *still*."

"One of these days you're going to ride in here and not ride out again."

"You've been telling me that for a long time."

"You mark my words, my friend. One of these days I'll be right."

Clint stuffed the telegram into his shirt pocket and said, "Just because you've met somebody and are ready to settle down, don't try and get me to do the same."

"Who says I'm ready to settle down?"

1. *THE GUNSMITH #3: THE WOMAN HUNT*

2. *THE GUNSMITH #22: BULLETS AND BALLOTS*

"Nobody says," Clint said, standing up. "It's in your voice when you talk about Jimmy's mother. What's her name?"

"Dorothy, Dorothy Kendrick."

"Well, you tell Dorothy I said hello."

"Where are you going?"

"To the livery stable to check on Duke."

"And then to your room?"

"Yeah."

"Where you've got one of my girls waiting?"

"Uh, I guess so, why?"

"Because every time you come back to town you end up in bed with one of my girls. Why is that?"

"Because," Clint said, "you're my friend, you know my type, and you keep hiring them."

Clint started for the door and Rick called out, "Gonna leave your rig behind?"

"Yeah, I guess. This is a social trip, so I won't be doing any work."

"When are you leaving?"

"In the morning."

"But you just got here yesterday."

"Hey," Clint said, walking back to thump his friend on the shoulder, "you know I don't like to stay anywhere long enough to put down roots."

"Yeah, I know," Rick said to himself as Clint left the saloon, "but this is ridiculous."

The girl this time was a redhead, freckles and all. She had freckles in the wide valley between her small breasts, freckles on her back, and freckles on the cheeks of her buttocks. With all these freckles, however, it was the rust-colored nipples that fascinated Clint Adams.

She was sitting astride him, riding him with his rigid penis deep inside of her, and he was sucking on her nipples, amazed at how distended they could become.

Her name was Lori—at least that's what he thought her name was.

When she was lying in the crook of his arm, momentarily satiated, her hand still on his semi-erect penis, he thought of what he'd said to Rick Hartman about hiring his type. He didn't have a type, really. He liked women in all shapes and sizes, and *that* was what Rick Hartman hired.

Women in all shapes and sizes.

This one was a tall, willowy redhead with freckles, and small breasts topped by wide, rust-colored nipples. The next one might be a short, voluptuous blonde with large breasts and pale skin.

It had almost become a game. Come to Labyrinth, see what kind of new girls Rick had hired, and then pick one.

Looking down at the face of the sleeping girl, he thought, What kind of game is this for a grown man to play?

When she woke up and attacked him with her mouth, he decided it wasn't such a bad game after all.

Chapter Two

Rio Malo's new sheriff left his office and headed for the café to have his first breakfast as the local lawman.

He'd only been on the job since the previous afternoon, after the ballots had been counted. The first order of business had been to send his friend Clint Adams a telegram telling him about the job. Clint had been with him the first time he'd ever run for sheriff, and lost—by five votes.[3] He hadn't tried again until now.

Of course, he didn't tell Clint in the telegram that he'd run unopposed. That might have taken a little of the luster away from the victory.

The previous sheriff, a man named Pete Banner, had decided not to run for office again. In fact, no one was going to run for office until Joe Bags—who had ridden into town only a week before—decided to try for the job. The town council had insisted on an election, requiring over fifty percent of the total vote to be in Bags's favor. If he hadn't gotten the required percentage, the office would have remained empty.

3. *THE GUNSMITH #22: BULLETS AND BALLOTS*

Of sixty-five votes cast, he had received thirty-three—winning the job by one vote. The other votes had been cast for various different names, and in most cases, simply for NO VOTE. This was out of the total town population of over six hundred.

Bags had the curious feeling that most of the people in this town didn't want a sheriff.

The feeling intensified as he walked through town toward the café. No one in the town greeted him, and many did not even look at him.

He wondered idly who the thirty-three people were who *had* voted for him . . . and why.

As he entered the café he saw the young waitress he'd been working on for a week, Nina Katrina. She was tall, dark-haired, and had a solid young body that he'd been thinking about since the first day he saw her.

Maybe now that he was sheriff . . .

"What are we gonna do about this new sheriff?" Dallas Tobin asked.

His father, John Tobin, regarded him across his desk and said, "What do we have to do about him?"

"I don't know."

"Then what did you ask for?"

"I don't know."

"That's your problem," John Tobin said, looking at his son distastefully. "You never know anything."

"Why are you always putting me down?" Dallas demanded angrily.

"Because you're not worth shit, that's why. Now get out of here and get to work."

"I'll show you," Dallas muttered, but he left the office without further word to his father.

John Tobin, at forty-eight, was a self-made man who took what he wanted all his life and built his ranch that way. His son Dallas, at twenty-one, had had it easy all his life. It was only recently that Tobin had forced Dallas to start working alongside the other hands.

It might have been too late though. The kid still thought he had everything coming to him easy—that was mostly due to his mother. But when she died three years ago, Tobin had to deal with the boy himself, and he'd chosen an entirely different manner.

He'd decided to try and make the boy into a man, and so far, he had failed.

When Nina Katrina brought Joe Bags—*Sheriff* Joe Bags—his breakfast, she asked, "Are you gonna pay for this?"

"Why wouldn't I?" he asked.

"I never knew a lawman yet who paid for his meals."

"Well, you're looking at one now."

She put the plate down and he caught a whiff of her—just her, no fancy perfume or anything. He liked it.

"Well, maybe you will be different," she said, straightening up, "although it's really too early to tell, isn't it?"

"If you spent more time on it, maybe you could find out sooner."

"I've got other people to serve," she said. She started away, then turned back. "How about some biscuits?"

"They come with the meal?"

"They're on the house."

"Will I make a bad impression if I say yes?"

"Don't worry about it," she said. "You started off on the right foot."

He watched her walk away and hoped that she was right.

When Dallas Tobin left his house—his *father's* house—he had no intentions of going to work.

Luke Joyner, his friend, was waiting for him outside with two horses.

"Are we going to town?"

Joyner was a big lad of twenty, six-three and two twenty at least. Dallas Tobin was a slim five-ten, and liked having Joyner with him.

"Yeah, Luke, we're going to town."

"We gonna see Nina?"

"Yup."

"Good."

Luke liked Nina Katrina, but he knew that Dallas liked her, too, so he settled for just looking at her. If anyone was going to touch, it would be his good friend Dallas.

Maybe, Luke thought, Dallas would let him watch that.

After Sheriff Joe Bags left, Nina Katrina moved to the window to watch him as he walked down the street. She was oddly attracted to him, and amused that he seemed to want to get to know her but didn't know how. It was just as well, she thought. The way Dallas Tobin felt about her—as if she belonged to him—striking up a relationship with the new sheriff would just start a lot of trouble that neither she nor the sheriff needed.

As she watched Bags walk away, she saw Dallas Tobin and his big friend, Luke, ride into town, and knew they would be coming there for dinner. She also knew that Dallas would want to share her bed that night, and knew she wouldn't dare refuse. The Tobins ran the town, and sleeping with the son was just her way of staying on the father's good side.

Of course, if she thought the new sheriff was man enough to stand against the Tobins . . .

Dallas Tobin and Luke Joyner tied their horses off and walked over to the café. Dallas stopped to look in the window and watch Nina walk from table to table. She just loved what he had between his legs for her, he thought, and he had every intention of giving it to her again tonight. She was better than any of the whores his father had out to the house, and she was one woman his father would never have.

She saved all her honey for Dallas Tobin.

Chapter Three

A week later Clint Adams rode into Rio Malo. He found a larger town than he'd thought. Joe Bags had not done badly for himself. Oh, it wasn't Dodge City, or even Labyrinth, Texas, but it was a good start for Joe.

Clint left Duke at the livery with the much impressed Mexican liveryman. He didn't need directions to the hotel because he'd passed it on the way.

After leaving his gear at the hotel he went in search of the saloon. It was after noon, and he'd been riding all morning and was ready for a cold beer.

As soon as he entered the Dancer House Saloon he saw the woman. The place was not doing a brisk business at that time of day, and she was seated at a back table. She had auburn hair and an unusual face. Her eyes were big and set widely apart, and her lips were of equal fullness. She looked up, saw him looking at her, and then looked down again. She seemed to be doing books, which meant she was either the manager or the owner.

He walked to the bar and ordered a beer. When the bartender brought it, he said, "I hear you've got a new sheriff in town."

"That's right." The bartender was a big, florid-faced man who looked bored.

"He any good?"

The big man shrugged, working the countertop with a dirty rag.

"Too soon to tell, huh?"

The big man shrugged again.

"Thanks for the information."

"Welcome," the man said, and went to the end of the bar to mop a nonexistent wet spot with his dirty rag.

Clint turned, holding his beer, and looked at the woman again. She was wearing a plain dress that buttoned all the way to her neck, but he could see the proud thrust of full, heavy breasts. When she stood up he imagined she would be very tall, almost his own height.

She was a lot of woman.

He finished the beer, set the empty mug down on the bar, and walked out. He'd return later, when the woman was not so occupied by business.

He stopped a man on the street and asked him to suggest a good place to have lunch. The man gave him directions to a café a block away.

The waitress was tall and dark-haired. She suggested steak: "It's the only thing besides breakfast that the cook doesn't burn."

"I'll take it then."

"How about some potatoes and biscuits?" she asked.

"Sounds fine."

"Say that after you've tasted it," she said.

"Is the coffee any good?"

"That's our specialty."

"Then bring me a pot now."

"Sure."

When she brought the coffee, he said, "I hear you've got a new sheriff in town."

"Yeah, we do."

"Is he any good?"

"He'd better be."

"Why do you say that?"

"Because he's on his own."

"No deputies, you mean?"

"That's what I mean."

"How come?"

"Being a deputy in this town ain't a healthy job."

"What about being a sheriff?"

"That's even worse."

"How's that?"

"Let me get your steak and I'll tell you."

She went into the kitchen and came back with his steak. There was enough blood in the plate with it to soak the biscuits in.

"So tell me."

"The Tobins run this town, Dallas and his father John. If the sheriff ain't in their pocket, then he's in for trouble."

"And this sheriff isn't in their pocket?"

"Not yet. If they can get him, then he may be all right, but if they can't . . ."

"What do you think?"

"I think he's too dumb to put himself in anyone's pocket."

"Sounds like an honest man."

She shrugged and said, "Same thing."

As she started away he asked, "Is he a friend of yours?"

"Sheriff Bags?" she asked, grinning slightly. "Oh, he'd like to be."

"What are his chances?"

"Slim," she said, "but then that's better than most."

As she walked away he watched her hips twitch and knew that Bags would be after this one. The one in the saloon wouldn't be his type. For one thing, she was older. For another, this one was pretty, while the other one was interesting looking. Clint found the lady in the saloon more attractive, but he'd been around longer than Bags and looked for different things in a woman.

This waitress was certainly worth taking a chance on though. He decided he'd have to find out how deep Bags's interest really went.

When she brought him his second pot of coffee, he asked, "Have you seen the sheriff around today?"

"He was in for breakfast, like always. I haven't seen him since, but then, I haven't been away from here."

"If you had to guess, where would you say he was?"

"Out looking for deputies, I guess. That's what he's been doing since he was voted in."

"I see."

She frowned at him and asked, "Why you asking so many questions about the new sheriff?"

"I'm here to see him. He's a friend of mine."

"Oh yeah?"

"I came to wish him luck in his new job."

"Well," she said, heading back to the kitchen, "he sure as hell is gonna need it."

Chapter Four

Joe Bags rode back into town about three in the afternoon. He'd hit some of the surrounding ranches, looking for potential deputies, and had come up empty. Of course, he'd avoided the Tobin spread. It was Tobin's men who made the sheriff's job as tough as it was in this town, and they were the reason he was going to need at least two deputies.

He put his horse up in the livery, and as he was about to leave, his eyes fell on a big black in one of the stalls.

"I don't believe it."

He walked up to the stall for a closer look at the black. It was a huge gelding who stared at him with a challenging look, as if it were daring the sheriff to come near him.

There was only one horse like that.

"Well, how you doing, Duke?" he asked, careful not to get too close to the big gelding.

"A stranger brought that horse in this afternoon, Sheriff," Manuel, the liveryman said. "You want I should describe him for you?"

"No, that's all right, Manuel. I know who the man is." He started to leave, then stopped and turned to the liveryman. Manuel was in his sixties, frail and sickly. "Manuel, you ever think of becoming a deputy?"

"Me, señor?" Manuel asked, looking shocked.

"No, you're right," Bags said, shaking his head. "Forget it. I'm just getting desperate."

Bags left the livery. First he wanted a drink, and then he wanted to find Clint Adams.

Maybe he'd find them both in the same place.

During the two hours that followed lunch, Clint met Gimpy Kane and Laramie Jones in Rio Malo's other, smaller saloon.

Gimpy Kane was a man in his fifties who carried a Greener shotgun with him wherever he went. He went by the name Gimpy because he had a gimpy leg. He was about five-eight, barrel-chested, and powerful looking, with a scarred face which had to have been well earned. Clint could only think of the man as an old warrior.

Clint saw him in the small saloon, and it was Kane who struck up the conversation. Eventually Clint bought him a drink, and discovering that Kane was not a resident of Rio Malo, sounded him out on the prospect of being a deputy sheriff.

"I don't live in this town," Kane reminded him, "I'm just passing through."

"Tell me you can't use a few extra dollars."

Kane laughed. "Every man can use a few extra dollars. The man that says he can't is a liar, but being a deputy is something I ain't never tried before. I don't know how good I'd be at it."

"You don't need to be too good at it," Clint assured him. "The sheriff here would just need you until he could find somebody permanent."

"Well . . ."

"Talk to him, at least. I'll introduce you later on."

"He a friend of yours?"

"He is."

"Why don't you take the job?"

"I, uh, have my reasons."

"Well, speaking of introducing people, how about introducing yourself? You said your name is Clint. What goes with that?"

"My name's Adams, Clint Adams."

"Adams, did you say?"

"Yes."

Kane had obviously recognized the name, but he did not make a big thing of it, which Clint liked.

"All right, Mr. Adams, I'll talk to your friend the sheriff. How about my partner?"

"Who's your partner?"

"The lad playing poker over there."

Clint looked over and saw three townsmen playing poker with a boy who seemed a teenager.

"The boy?"

"I know he looks about eighteen or so, but he's twenty-six, and he can use a gun."

"Would he be interested in a job as a deputy?"

"He would be if I was."

"Is he your son?"

"Naw, we ain't kin, we just ride together. He'll talk to your sheriff friend too. Seems to me if he can use one temporary deputy, he could use two."

"All right," Clint said. "Now all I've got to do is find him."

"When you do, we'll be right here."

"I'll try the other saloon."

"I hear that one's owned by a woman, a right good-looking woman."

"I think I saw her."

"She purty?"

"Very."

Kane downed a whiskey and signaled the bartender to pour him another. "Women can run whorehouses, but I never knew one yet could run a saloon right."

"I'll let you know what I think of this one."

"The saloon or the woman?" Kane asked with a lewd grin.

"Both."

"We'll be here."

Clint left the smaller saloon and headed for the other, larger one run by the woman he'd seen earlier. Even if he didn't find Bags there, maybe he would find out the woman's name.

And more.

Chapter Five

Joe Bags was standing at the bar when Clint Adams entered April Dancer's saloon. There was no one standing near him, as if he had a bad cold, or the plague.

Clint walked up to him, and the two men stared at each other.

"Been a few years," Clint finally said.

"You got older."

"And I suppose you're wearing your hat like that because your hair isn't thinning?"

Bags's hat was pulled down lower than Clint remembered him wearing it. Bags reached for it, then pulled his hand away and laughed.

"It's in my genes. My pa was bald when he was thirty." Bags stuck his hand out and Clint shook it.

"Hope you don't mind, but I thought I'd come and congratulate you in person."

"Congratulations may not be in order," Bags said. "I've been having a little trouble coming up with deputies."

"So I've heard."

"Bartender, give my friend a drink."

"Is he paying?" the bartender asked.

21

"I'm paying," Sheriff Bags said.

"What'll you have?"

"A beer."

The bartender put a mug of beer on the bar and Bags paid for it. The bartender was more than a little surprised.

"Jesus, here and at the café," Bags said, leading Clint to a table. "You'd think they never saw a man with a badge pay for anything before."

"They probably haven't."

They sat down and Clint leaned back and made a big show of studying Sheriff Joe Bags.

"How does it look?" Bags asked, glancing down at the badge on his chest.

"Could use a spit shine, otherwise I guess it looks all right."

"Got a dent in it, but that gives it character, I figure."

"I guess so."

"What do you think of the town?"

"Haven't been here long enough to form an opinion."

"That's probably what people are saying about me."

"It is. I've been asking around since I got here this afternoon."

"Who'd you ask?"

"A few people here and there. Waitress over at the café—"

"Nina?"

"Is that her name?"

"Long dark hair, real pretty face, body like a—"

"That's her," Clint said, enjoying the faraway

look that came into Bags's eyes when he talked about the waitress.

"What did she say about me?" Bags asked eagerly.

Clint shrugged. "She said it was too soon to tell. She's the one who told me you were having trouble getting deputies."

"She's got that right."

"Also told me something about a man named Tobin."

"Which one?"

"That's right, she did mention two of them."

"John and his boy Dallas. John Tobin's a big man hereabouts, Clint, and his boy thinks that entitles him to do whatever he wants—him and his friends."

"And the old man backs him up?"

"I don't know what the old man does—although he's not that old. Just a little older than you, as a matter of fact. Anyway, he hardly ever comes to town, just stays on that ranch of his."

"Has he got a wife?"

"The way I hear it, she died some years back. I know he has a woman brought out there from time to time, from Jenny Lee's whorehouse."

"Well, at least the town's got a cathouse," Clint said. "That shows some inkling of civilization. How many people in Rio Malo?"

"Six hundred or so."

"You must have impressed most of them in the short time you were here in order to get elected."

"I was hoping you wouldn't bring that up."

"Why?"

Bags told Clint about running unopposed and

24

about the meager turnout at the polls.

"Sounds like a town that doesn't want a sheriff."

"I guess they figure to let Dallas Tobin and his friends do what he pleases. Having a sheriff stand in his way would only cause more trouble."

"Anybody from the town council talk to you?"

"Not a one."

"They have a town council?"

"Oh, they got one, all right, but I ain't seen hide nor hair of any of 'em since I took office."

"Sounds to me like you're on your own."

"You got that right."

"Sounds to me like you better saddle up and leave here with me."

"Nooo, Clint, no way," Bags said, putting his beer down. He touched his sheriff's star and said, "This is my first sheriff's star, and I intend to wear it for a while."

"Then you're going to need deputies."

"That brings us back to where I started," Bags said, picking up his mug again. "Nobody wants to stand against the Tobins."

"I wouldn't say no one."

"Who'd you have in mind?"

"Somebody who has the same qualities you have."

"You mean you found someone in this town who is brave, courageous, strong, and honest?"

"Nope," Clint said, "I found two strangers."

Chapter Six

Clint and Bags left the Dancer House and headed for the other saloon, where Clint supposed that Gimpy Kane was still drinking and Laramie Jones still playing poker.

"Where did you find these fellas?"

"I was just having a drink at the bar and this fella started talking to me. When I found out he was just passing through town, he seemed a likely candidate for a deputy. Turns out he's got a partner, so that makes two."

"Are they any good?"

"I guess we'll have to find that out. Kane carries a Greener with him and claims that Laramie Jones is a hand with a gun."

"What kind of a name is Gimpy?"

"He's got a gimpy leg."

"A gimp and a kid."

"The kid's twenty-six, and how much older than that are you?"

"Old enough."

"Tell me something about the woman who runs the Dancer House," Clint said, changing the subject.

"You saw her, huh?"

"Earlier today."

"Her name's April Dancer, and I don't know what a woman like her is doing in this town."

"That's what I was thinking."

"Anyway, she owns and operates the Dancer House and is apparently a force in this town. She has a seat on the town council, and I understand that John Tobin and she are old friends."

"Does that mean what it implies?"

"I wasn't implying anything," Bags said, "I was just repeating what I heard."

They reached the smaller saloon and suspended conversation about April Dancer.

"There he is," Clint said, seeing Gimpy Kane still standing at the bar.

"Let's go and meet him."

Bags started forward, but Clint noticed something developing and put his hand on his arm.

"What's wrong?"

"You wanted to find out if they were any good?"

"Sure."

"Let's just watch then."

"Wha—"

"Something's happening here. Let's watch. Get behind me so nobody sees your badge."

Bags moved behind Clint and both men watched what was happening.

Gimpy Kane was standing at the bar, his Greener held in the crook of his left arm while he drank his beer with his right. Clint had seen the three men at the other end of the bar watching Kane, nudging each other and whispering, and knew that they were going to try the old warrior. He checked the poker game and saw Laramie Jones still playing, but not unaware of what was going on. That spoke well for the younger man, he thought.

The three men pushed away from the bar and sashayed down toward Gimpy Kane, who was seemingly unaware of their approach. One went past Kane while the other two stopped on the older man's right. All three men were of a type—young, cocky, full of themselves, confident that they could get away with anything they wanted to.

"Did you see this old feller limp on in here, Cass?" one of the men asked the other.

"I sure did. Looked like he needed one of them there wheelchairs."

The two men who were speaking were on Kane's right. The man on his left remained silent, and alert.

"Hey, Pop," the first man said, "would you like us to get you one of them wheelchairs?"

Kane didn't answer. As he started to lift his beer to his lips the man leaned over and jostled his arm. Beer spilled down Kane's shirt front.

"Hey, look, the cripple's got a crippled hand too. You want us to hold your beer for you, cripple?"

Clint studied Laramie Jones, who looked for all the world like a man totally engrossed in a poker game. He even snapped at the other players to make their bets and stop looking around.

"Hey, cripple, I'm talking to you!"

In response to the man's new tone, Kane turned his head and looked at him.

"Are you talking to me?"

"Yeah, I'm talking to you. Do you see another cripple around here?" The man looked to his friend for approval, and his friend nodded.

"Not yet I don't," Kane said in answer to the

question, "but you're coming pretty close."

"What?" the man said, as if he hadn't heard straight.

Kane looked at the bartender and said, "Get me another beer and put it on my friend's bill."

"I ain't your friend, old man," the man said, "and I ain't buying you a beer."

"Why don't you take your friend and go home," Kane said. "Don't push me."

"I'll do worse than push you, old man," the other man said. "I'll cut you."

With that he went for a knife he was wearing on his hip. Kane moved so fast Clint could hardly follow him. The Greener came out of the crook of his arm upside down and the stock struck the first man on the butt of the jaw. He dropped his knife and slumped to the floor. His friend went for his gun, but before he could reach it, the twin barrels of the Greener were wedged under his chin, the hammers cocked.

The third man, the one behind Kane, drew his gun slowly, and Clint was about to move when Laramie Jones stood, drew, and fired. His bullet smacked into the third man's upper arm, causing him to drop his gun. Kane never even turned around. Jones holstered his gun and sat back down. He'd never let go of his cards, which he held in his left hand.

"Let's play cards," he said.

"Okay, Sheriff," Clint said to Bags, stepping aside, "do your job."

Chapter Seven

Bags removed everyone to his office: Kane, Jones, and the three hardcases. He tossed the three men into a cell and had the town doctor patch up the arm of the injured one.

After the doctor left, Bags looked at Kane and Jones, who were sitting with their legs outstretched—that is, three of their legs were outstretched. The fourth one, Kane's gimpy leg, wouldn't ever stretch again, but it did the best it could.

Clint was standing in a corner, watching Bags.

"All right, Clint tells me you two want to be deputies."

Clint closed his eyes but remained quiet. Maybe Bags would salvage it after all.

"That's not strictly true," Laramie Jones said. "At least that was not the impression I got from my colleague's side of the story."

"Oh?"

"Your friend asked my friend if he was interested in being a deputy. My friend told your friend that he would talk to you about it. My friend also told your friend that I would talk to you about it." Jones looked over at *his* friend and asked, "Have I got this right?"

"Absolutely."

Bags looked at Clint, who looked away.

"All right, I put it the wrong way. Let me say it another way. I would appreciate it very much if you two would hire on as temporary deputies until I can come up with somebody steady. What do you say?"

Jones looked at Kane, who said, "He did ask nice, didn't he?"

"I guess." Jones looked at Bags and said, "What does it pay?"

"I wish you hadn't asked that. . . ."

"What do you think?" Clint asked Bags after Kane and Jones had left.

"They'll do, I guess."

"They'll do? If you're lucky, you might get them to stay for good."

"No," Bags said, shaking his head. "I don't like the kid, and Kane's gimp might cost him somewhere along the line."

"Beggars shouldn't be choosy, Bags."

"I'm not a beggar."

"You need deputies, so you can't afford to be proud at this point. These two will do until something else comes along."

"Sure I can't persuade you to put on a badge?"

"I don't think so, Bags, but I'll stay around for a while."

"Want to get a drink?"

"Sure. Let's go to the Dancer House."

"Looking to meet April Dancer, huh?"

"Yes."

"What about these three?"

"Let's wait until your two deputies get back."

"If they come back. They didn't look too happy about having to stay in the office to watch these three."

"Why not?" Clint asked. "They actually put them here, didn't they?"

"What are we doing taking a nothing-paying job like deputies in a one-horse town like this?" Laramie Jones asked Gimpy Kane.

"It might be interesting."

Kane and Jones were in their hotel room which, as deputy sheriff's of Rio Malo, they were no longer paying for.

"We're getting this room for nothing, you know."

"Great. Now we have to go back to the sheriff's office and baby-sit those three cowboys."

Kane shrugged and said, "We put them there."

"You're right," Jones said. "We should have just killed them."

"That's not the way a deputy is supposed to think."

"Excuse me, but I haven't had that much experience being a deputy. Do I get to keep playing poker?"

"I don't see why not. Lawmen play poker. Look at the sheriff's friend."

"The sheriff's friend. That's all you ever call him—'the sheriff's friend.' How about telling me who he is?"

"Why?"

"Because there's got to be another reason you wanted to take this job. What's his name?"

"Adams, Clint Adams."

"Adams?" Jones said. He'd been lying on the bed, and now he sat up and brought his feet down to the floor with a bang. "The Gunsmith?"

"The same."

"You know," Laramie Jones said after a few moments, "this might be interesting."

Del Wilson had been in the small saloon when Kane and Jones had taken care of the three young hardcases. He'd watched as the new sheriff took everyone to his office and then let the gimp and his partner go free. He had also heard the doctor talking after he'd treated the injured man and gone to the saloon for a drink.

That was how he found out that the new sheriff now had two deputies.

Del Wilson worked on the Tobin ranch and was one of Dallas Tobin's friends.

He rode to the Tobin ranch that evening to tell Dallas the news.

Chapter Eight

This time when Clint and Bags entered the Dancer House, Bags was noticed as the sheriff. A space opened at the bar for him, and he and Clint moved into it.

"Beer, Sheriff?" the bartender asked.

"Two."

Kane and Jones had returned to the office and been left in charge of the three prisoners.

"What do we do for dinner?" Laramie Jones had asked.

"I'll bring something back for you, don't worry."

As they left the office Bags had said, "I still don't like the kid."

"The kid," Clint mimicked. "You're making yourself an old man before your time."

"I'll never see thirty again."

"You're a lot closer to forty than thirty, so stop pushing it."

Now, standing at the bar, Clint reflected on how he hadn't yet seen Bags without his hat. The younger man had never been the proud possessor of a bushy head of hair, and it seemed that now he was trying to hide what was left.

That can make a man feel older than he is, he thought, cause him to be in enough of a hurry to take the wrong job in the wrong place just because it was there to be had.

"There she is," Bags said.

Clint looked in the mirror and saw that April Dancer had just entered the room—a different April Dancer than he had seen earlier. This one was wearing a gown cut low over a swelling bosom, and hair piled high on her head to reveal a smooth, graceful neck. Her face was skillfully made up, and where her face had been interesting, it was now absolutely beautiful. Her big eyes were still widely set, and her full mouth, carefully painted, looked like a lush piece of fruit just begging to be bitten.

As marvelous as she looked now, Clint found that he preferred the more sedate April he'd seen working on the books instead of the customers.

"Jesus, look at her," Bags said, staring at her in open admiration.

"Going off your waitress?"

Bags looked at him and said, "Nina? Hell, no. I mean, April's beautiful, but she's more your type, not mine."

"You mean she's closer to my age than yours?"

Bags grinned and said, "Aren't you the one telling me not to get old before my time?"

"I know, but she can't be a day older than . . . thirty-five."

"Nina's about twenty-six, Clint. You take April, and I'll take Nina."

Clint looked at April, walking around the room, stopping here and there to talk to someone or lay a hand on someone's shoulder, and said, "You've got a deal there."

April worked her way around the whole room and eventually got to where the new sheriff was standing with his friend.

"Sheriff, welcome to Dancer House."

"Thank you, Miss Dancer."

"I hope you'll be doing most of your drinking here. It never hurts to have a lawman around."

"Miss Dancer, this is my friend, Clint Adams."

"Mr. Adams."

"Miss Dancer."

"Are you one of the sheriff's deputies, Mr. Adams?"

"No, ma'am. The sheriff and I are old friends. I just came into town to wish him well in his new position."

"Well, we all wish him well. This town could use a good lawman."

"Seems like a nice, friendly town to me."

"Stay around for a while," she said. "Every town has its ugly face."

"Looking at you, I can't imagine this town ever looking ugly."

"Ah, you're a nice talker, Mr. Adams."

"Call me Clint, please."

She grinned and said, "Clint." She leaned over and said into his ear, "I eat nice talkers for breakfast," and continued on.

"What did she say?" Bags asked.

"I'm not sure," Clint said, looking after her with interest, "something about breakfast. Come on, let's have another beer and then get some dinner."

• • •

When Sheriff Bags walked in with his friend, Nina Katrina wasn't too happy. She knew that Dallas Tobin was coming in shortly with his friend Luke, and the kid was coming in to get her. She didn't want Bags there to see her leave with him. With the place empty, she wouldn't be able to slip out without him seeing.

"Hello, Nina," Bags said as he and his friend sat down.

"Hello, Sheriff."

"What's good tonight?"

"Not much," she said. "As a matter of fact I was thinking of closing up early."

That was Clint's first inkling that Nina Katrina was something more than just a waitress. Apparently she either partly or solely owned the café.

He also noticed that she didn't seem to want them around at that moment.

"Come on, Joe, we can eat somewhere else."

"Wait, Clint. I'm sure Nina has something left in the kitchen."

"I really don't have much, Sheriff—"

"Whatever you have will be fine, Nina. It's sure to be better than anything we could get anywhere else."

"Joe—"

Clint stopped when the door opened and two men walked in. One was young, about twenty, and the other no older, but a lot bigger. He was, in fact, one of the biggest men Clint had ever seen.

Clint saw Nina look at them, and she became very nervous.

"Nina," the smaller man called. "Come on, let's go, woman."

Bags looked at the man who was speaking, then at Nina. "That's Dallas Tobin," he said.

"I know."

"What's he want with you?"

"Sheriff, it's closing time," she said, taking off her apron.

"What about the cook?" Clint asked.

"I'm the cook, I'm the waitress," she said. "I have to close."

"Hey," Dallas Tobin said, coming closer. "Is that our new sheriff?" He turned to his friend and said, "Hey, Luke, that's our new sheriff."

"I see."

"Did I interrupt you and your friend's dinner, Sheriff?"

"We didn't even get a chance to order," Clint said. He didn't like the way Bags was looking from Nina to Dallas Tobin.

"Well, I'm really sorry, then, but I just came for my girl and she's got to close."

"Your girl?" Bags asked.

Tobin looked at Bags and said, "That's right, Sheriff, my girl. Didn't she tell you?"

"No . . ." Bags said, looking at Nina. "She didn't tell me."

"Come on now, Sheriff," Tobin said, "be a good lad and find someplace else to eat."

As Tobin called Bags "lad," Clint saw a fire light in Bags's eyes. Before he could stop him, Bags stood up and went nose to nose with Tobin, who—backed by his big friend—didn't take a backward step.

"Bags . . ."

Bags looked at Nina and said, "Do you want to go with him?"

Nina looked at Tobin and was tempted right there and then to see if Bags was man enough to handle him and Joyner. But she was only tempted.

"Yes, Sheriff. I want to go with him. Now, please leave so I can close."

Bags turned and looked at Tobin, who had a self-satisfied smirk on his face.

Clint knew that Bags was going to make a mistake, so he stood up and grabbed his friend by the shoulders. "Come on, Sheriff. We've got to find someplace else to eat before they close. We've got deputies to feed."

"Deputies," Tobin said as Clint pulled Bags toward the door. "A gimp and a poker-playing kid."

Dallas Tobin seemed to think that his father's power belied his years, that at twenty or so he could call men older than him "lad" and "kid" in a derisive manner.

"Tobin, remember one thing," Bags said. "I'm the law in this town. You and your friends better remember that. I don't want any of your boys to step out of line, because I'll knock them right back into line."

"Does that go for Luke, too, Sheriff?" Tobin asked, smiling.

Bags looked at Luke Joyner and said, "Yeah, that goes for him too—and especially for you."

"Sheriff, you'd be well advised to make this the shortest term of any sheriff in history. Just take off the badge and ride out."

"Remember what I said, Tobin. I don't care who you are or who your father is. Toe the line in my town."

Bags allowed Clint to usher him out the door, and Joyner took two steps as if to follow.

"Forget it, Luke. He'll find out soon enough whose town this is."

Tobin turned to Nina and said, "Come on, gal. Let's get moving." Grabbing himself by the crotch he said, "I got something for you you're just gonna love."

Chapter Nine

"Do you believe that?" Bags demanded.

They were in another café, waiting for the dinners they had ordered for Gimpy Kane and Laramie Jones. As soon as they got them, this café would also close.

"Nina and Dallas Tobin," Bags said in disbelief.

"Take it easy, Joe."

"You take it easy. You didn't have some kid with a rich daddy telling you that your girl was his."

"*Your* girl?"

"She would have been, if I had enough time."

"You've got all the time in the world, Joe. You don't think she wants to be with him, do you?"

"She said she did, didn't she?"

"Put yourself in her place. A waitress in a little New Mexico town, is she going to stand up to the son of the richest man in the county and say she doesn't want him?"

"Then why did she say—"

"She needs somebody to stand with her against them, Bags. Is that you?"

"It could be."

"You've got a job to do. You can't let personal feelings get in the way."

"Who says I can't? Don't tell me you never let your feelings get in the way."

"I never claimed to be the best lawman in the country—"

"And neither do I," Bags said. The waiter came with the two dinners, and Bags took them and turned to leave without paying. "If she needs my help, she's gonna get it. *That's* my job, ain't it?"

Clint shrugged, said, "That's your job," and followed him out.

Nina Katrina studied the ceiling while Dallas Tobin busied himself between her legs. It was disgusting, the noises he made when he was licking at her, sucking her. He was eating her as if she were a bowl of soup, slurping and gulping—and he thought she liked it!

In truth she had liked it in the beginning—hell, sex felt good no matter who you had it with—but as time went on it stopped being sex. It was a chore to lie in bed with him and listen to the noises he made. In the beginning she never had to fake her reactions, but lately she did, and he never knew the difference.

She faked it now, lifting her hips off the bed, and he rolled away, licking his lips and smiling.

"You like that, huh? Don't you?"

"Sure, Dallas, sure."

They were in her room, which was right above the café she owned.

"Give me a second and then I'll give you something else you'll like."

"Sure, Dallas."

This was the last time, she swore to herself, absolutely the last time.

Sure.

That's what she had said last time.

After they brought the meals to Kane and Jones, Bags and Clint went their separate ways.

Bags's appetite had been ruined by what happened at Nina's café, and he said he was going to his room in the boardinghouse. The room came with the job.

Clint, whose appetite was intact, went to the Dancer House, because he remembered that the bar had a couple of stacks of sandwiches on it.

Maybe there'd be some left.

Chapter Ten

As Clint entered the Dancer House he saw that April Dancer had taken up a position at the end of the bar. She had a shot glass of whiskey in front of her.

He went to the bar, found a spot, elbowed his way in and ordered a beer.

"Got any of those sandwiches left?" Clint asked. He had to talk loudly to be heard above the din. The activity in the saloon was in full swing.

"We've been real busy tonight."

"Does that mean no?"

The bartender nodded.

"We might have some hard boiled eggs."

"Anything."

The bartender went to the end of the bar and spoke briefly to April Dancer. She looked down the bar at Clint, said something to the bartender, then walked down the bar holding her drink.

"I understand you're hungry?"

He turned to look at her. Up close she was devastating, her eyes and her scent especially. The eyes were so big a man could get lost in them, and her scent was titillating, to say the least. It was subtle,

45

but it invaded a man's senses.

"Starving."

"No dinner tonight?"

"I guess I waited too long, and all the cafés and restaurants closed."

"Are you willing to settle for some scrambled eggs and ham?"

"The bartender said hard-boiled eggs."

"Well, I'm the boss here, and I say we can do better . . . if you'd care to join me in my private dining room."

"Lead the way, lovely lady."

"Whiskey or coffee?" she asked.

"Coffee."

She reached past him to put her glass down, and her hair tickled his nose. She made a sign to the bartender and then turned to Clint. "Follow me, please."

She walked across the saloon floor and a path opened up like magic. Clint followed in her wake, and the path closed up again behind them. She was the Queen Bee here, and everyone treated her as such.

What, he wondered, did she want with him, all of a sudden? Well, if she was willing to feed him, he thought, he was willing to listen.

She led him to a door in the back wall, and when she opened it and he followed her through, he found that she did indeed have her own private dining room. There was a desk in a far corner, which illustrated that the room also doubled as an office.

A young black woman wearing an apron was busily setting two places at a good-sized wooden table with a highly polished finish.

"Please, take a seat, Mr. Adams."

"I thought we settled on Clint earlier," he said, seating himself at one end of the table. "Remember? That was when you told me you'd eat me for breakfast?"

"I remember."

April Dancer seated herself at the other end. "I suppose that means you had better call me April."

The black girl reappeared with a large pot of coffee and two cups on a tray, and poured them each a cup.

"That's excellent," Clint said, taking a taste. "That may be the best coffee I've ever had."

"You know good coffee when you taste it," she said, complimenting him. "I have it specially mixed and brewed for me."

"You wouldn't be looking for a husband, would you?"

"I'm afraid not."

He put his cup down and asked, "Then what are you looking for?"

"Right now, a late dinner. Sarah, do we have steak?"

"Yes, ma'am."

"Well, it seems I can offer steak and eggs instead of ham."

"That's fine."

Sarah left, leaving the coffeepot within Clint's reach, not her mistress's.

"Shall we talk while we're waiting, or is it possible I might say something that would cost me this wonderful meal?"

"I promised you a meal and you'll get it, no matter what happens here."

"Then what is it you want, Miss Dancer?"

"April."

"April."

"I'm interested in your friend."

"The sheriff?"

"Yes. What kind of man is he?"

"Headstrong."

"Will he make a good sheriff?"

"I hope so."

"Will he stand and fight if things get rough?"

"Yes. I told you he was headstrong."

"That could work for him or against him."

"I agree."

"Will you be staying in town long, or did you just come to congratulate him and recruit deputies for him?"

"I came to congratulate him, but I've seen some things hereabouts that have convinced me that an extended stay might be interesting."

"Am I to understand that I am included in that statement?"

"Well, either you or whoever blends this coffee for you," he said, sipping again. "Now suppose you tell me why my friend Joe Bags interests you, and why I interest you."

"Well, you interest me for obvious reasons. Your reputation."

"Which reputation is that?"

"Your gun."

"Oh, that one," he said with distaste.

"Have you another?"

"I thought you meant my sparkling personality. I am rather well known for that in some areas."

She looked amused. "I wasn't aware of that," she said, "but I suppose if you stay around long enough,

I may come to know that reputation as well."

Clint was about to reply when Sarah entered carrying a tray. On it were two steaming plates of steak, eggs, potatoes, and a third plate with freshly baked biscuits. It must have been heavy, yet she handled it with obvious ease.

"Perhaps we should suspend our discussion until after we've eaten," April said as Sarah set their plates down in front of them.

"I'm glad you feel that way, April," he said. "This looks like a meal that would require one's full attention."

Chapter Eleven

After dinner Sarah brought in a fresh pot of coffee, poured two cups, and left the pot within Clint's reach.

"You've impressed Sarah."

"How can you tell that?"

"Whenever I have a guest for dinner, she usually leaves the pot within my reach."

"If you'd like another cup, I'll be glad to come over there and pour it for you."

"I'm still working on this one, thank you."

"If it isn't too much trouble, then, could we get to the point of this feast?"

"John Tobin."

"I beg your pardon?"

"He's the point of this feast."

"What has John Tobin got to do with me?"

"Well, not so much with you as with your friend. As the new sheriff he's going to have a lot to do with John Tobin and Dallas Tobin."

"He's already had a run-in with Dallas Tobin."

"Oh?"

"They've already managed to establish ground for a personal grudge."

"That's interesting. I'm concerned with whether or not your friend and his deputies—and you, for as long as you're here—will be able to stand against the Tobins and their men."

"Why?"

"Well, it would be in my best interests to find someone who *could* successfully stand against them."

"Why is that?"

She regarded him silently for a few moments, then seemed to make a decision. "Tobin owns a piece of the Dancer House."

"John?"

"Yes."

"How did that come about?"

"I needed money to start it, and he invested."

"You haven't paid him back?"

"I've been trying, but there's interest involved. As successful as my business has been, I haven't been able to build up enough capital to pay the loan off in full."

"And if Tobin ran afoul of the law and was driven from the area, you wouldn't have to."

"It's crossed my mind. Actually, he's run afoul of the law many times, but we've never had a lawman he didn't own."

"You have now."

"But for how long? That's what I'm concerned with."

"Bags won't be bought, if that's what you're worried about."

"How do you know?"

"I know Bags. He's too stubborn to be bought,

and besides that, he's got a vested interest in seeing the Tobins taken care of."

"You mentioned something about that before. What's this vested interest?"

"He and Dallas are after the same woman."

"Nina Katrina?"

"You know about her?"

"I know she's been submitting to Dallas. We've spoken about it."

"You're friends?"

"Not exactly, but we have something in common."

"What's that?"

"At one time or another in our lives we've both submitted to Tobin men."

"She to Dallas, and you to . . ."

"To John, yes. There was a time when we were lovers . . . and there was a time when I thought we were in love. Neither lasted very long."

"And now you're business partners."

"Yes."

"And you want to be rid of him."

"Yes."

"From what I hear, Tobin's got a major spread. He'd be a fool to abandon that, or to get himself into a position where he would have to."

"All I want is him out of my life."

"Well, April," Clint said, standing up, "I thank you for the late dinner."

"Will you help me?"

"Help you what? You haven't made a specific request of me yet."

"I want you to make sure your friends can resist

Tobin before you leave town.''

"I see. You don't want me to take an active part then.''

"Well, certainly it wouldn't hurt. I could even make it worth your while.''

"Now, April,'' he said, scolding her, "how could you have any confidence in my helping Bags resist being bought by Tobin if I were to allow myself to be bought by you?''

April stood up and came around the table to stand close to Clint. "I wasn't talking about money.''

Clint put his arms around her and pulled her tight, so her full breasts were crushed against him. The heat of her body seemed to enter him and center on his groin. She had to be aware of the bulge pressing against her as well.

"I wouldn't let you do that, April.''

"Why not?''

"Because then it wouldn't mean any more than it did between you and John Tobin. The first time we're together, it's going to mean something.''

He released her, but she stayed pressed against him for a moment before backing off.

"I'll be in town awhile,'' he said, moving toward the door. "Why don't we just wait and see what develops. Okay?''

"Sure, Clint,'' she said, looking at him oddly, "sure. We'll see what develops.''

"Thanks for dinner.''

After Clint Adams left, April Dancer sat down in her seat, experiencing a rush of sexual appetite she hadn't had in a long time. She'd offered herself to the Gunsmith—and he had turned her down! It had been a long time since she made a bold offer like that, but even longer since a man had refused to take her up on it.

She'd been hoping to use Clint Adams—and his friend, the new sheriff—to her own advantage, but she was starting to want Clint Adams in an entirely different way.

Clint went to his hotel, removed his gun belt and boots, and reclined on the bed.

He could still feel April Dancer's breasts pressed against his chest, could still feel the heat that emanated from her body. The erection that had popped up when he'd pulled her against him had persistently refused to go down. He was starting to wonder if he hadn't made a mistake by not accepting her offer and taking her right there and then on that polished wood table.

It was times like this that he wondered why he didn't break with his long policy of not paying for sex. A whore's mouth right at that moment would have made his decision easier to live with.

Chapter Twelve

The next morning Clint walked over to Joe Bags's office and found the new sheriff asleep at his desk, head down in his arms.

"Hey!"

Bags lifted his head in reply to the shout, eyes wide and momentarily unseeing.

"Time to get up."

Slowly, Bags focused his eyes on Clint, then rubbed his face with both hands.

"You didn't sleep here all night, did you?"

"Yeah, I did. Make some coffee, will you?"

By the time Clint had a pot of coffee grounds boiling on the potbellied stove, Joe Bags had used a pitcher and basin to wash up and had put on a clean shirt. When he returned to his desk he found a hot, black cup of coffee waiting for him.

"Thanks."

"Why'd you come back here last night?"

"I figured I'd spring my two new deputies. They probably had things they wanted to do, and I didn't."

"Joe—"

"What do you think of my cutting those three loose today?"

"It's up to you. You can hold them over for trial, if you like."

"No, I figured I'd fine them and run them out of town."

"Fine."

Bags sipped his coffee, made a face, then said, "That's strong!"

"That's as good as it gets with what I had at hand." It certainly couldn't compare with the special blend that April Dancer had given him the night before.

Bags took the keys to the cell, went into the back and released the three men. Clint watched as he levied a fine on the three and told them they either paid it or spent thirty days in jail. They produced the money, and when Bags told them to ride out of town, they told him not to worry, they couldn't get out fast enough to suit them.

"Very well done," Clint said after they'd left.

"Yeah," Bags said. He picked up the coffee, sipped it, made a face, then drank some more. "It grows on you after a couple of sips."

"Listen," Clint said, taking a seat, "I had a very interesting late dinner with April Dancer last night."

"Oh, really? If you're gonna come in here and tell me about your latest conquest, I ain't exactly in the mood to hear it."

"No conquest. We talked business."

"What kind of business?"

Clint related to Bags the conversation that took place before and after dinner.

"What did you talk about during dinner?"

"We were too busy eating to talk."

He also told Bags about her offer to him.

"And you turned her down?"

"I got scruples."

"What do you have to take to cure that?"

"I mean, when I go to bed with her, I want it to be for the right reasons, not because she's looking to buy me."

"You must have gone to bed in pain."

"Tell me about it."

"A whore could have fixed that up right quick. You still ain't paying for it?"

"I'm still not paying for it."

Bags rubbed his jaw and said, "You must have had a lot of painful nights in your life."

"I didn't see you hot footing it to the cathouse last night."

"I was angry. I would have been angry going in, and I still would have been angry coming out."

"Are you still angry?"

"I'm disappointed, but I thought about what you said, and now I'm thinking about what April said to you."

"And?"

"And maybe this whole town needs somebody to stand up to the Tobins."

"And that's going to be you?'

"No, it's going to be us."

"Us?"

"Us," Bags repeated. "Me, my deputies . . . and you. Could I have some more coffee, please?"

"Get it yourself."

Bags got up, poured himself a cup, then brought the pot over to Clint and poured him another cup.

"You did tell her that you were going to stay around for awhile, didn't you?"

"I did."

"Want to make that stay with a badge?"

"I do not."

"You're a stubborn man."

"I am."

Bags put the pot back on the stove and sat behind his desk. "I don't think we'll have to wait long for Dallas Tobin to pull something."

"Not after yesterday. Are you willing to wait for him to make the first move?"

"I've got to, don't I? I mean, I'm the law, I can't very well go after him."

"Well, you're learning."

"You know, when this whole thing does start, you won't have an official standing."

"That's okay," Clint said. "I have friends in high places."

"Is that a fact?"

"Mmm-hmm. I know the sheriff."

"Ha! That and two bits will get you a beer."

Chapter Thirteen

Dallas Tobin and Luke Joyner were holding court in the barn on the Tobin ranch. The other six men in the barn were their friends, and all looked to Dallas for leadership. After all, he *was* the boss's son.

"You probably have all heard that we have a new sheriff in town."

There was a rumble of agreement.

"Is he in your daddy's pocket?" one man asked.

"Not that I know of, but I'm sure my father will be working on that. We, on the other hand, will be working on the new sheriff in a different way."

"What way is that?" someone asked.

"We're gonna make him turn tail and run."

"How we gonna do that?"

"We're gonna make being the sheriff of Rio Malo look like the toughest job in the world."

"How we gonna do that?" the same man asked.

Looking annoyed, Dallas Tobin said, "You fellas are just gonna do whatever I tell you to do. . . ."

John Tobin stared across the desk at his foreman, Simon Trehayne. Trehayne had ridden with Tobin twenty years ago, when they had first come to New

Mexico, but not as partners, since Trehayne had always recognized Tobin's leadership abilities. When Tobin started his spread, he'd offered Trehayne a partnership and Trehayne had refused, settling instead for the job of foreman.

"It's a job I can do well," he had said, and thus far he had been true to his word.

"What do we know about this new sheriff?" Tobin asked.

Trehayne shrugged. "He's been sheriff for a week and he's spent most of that time looking for deputies."

"I heard that he found two."

"Yeah, strangers. A gimp and a kid."

"They any good?"

"They had a set-to with three drifters in one of the saloons last night and gave a pretty good account of themselves."

"Will they be trouble?"

"The way I read them, they can probably be bought."

"What about the sheriff?"

"There's another factor."

"Which is?"

"Clint Adams."

"The Gunsmith?"

Trehayne nodded. "He's in town, and apparently he and the sheriff are old friends."

"Has the sheriff made him a deputy?"

"No."

"Then he has no official standing."

"No."

"All right. Until he does, we'll simply work

around him. Make the usual offer to the sheriff and see what he says."

"All right."

"What has my son been up to?"

"Visiting that waitress of his."

Tobin made a face.

"There may be a problem there too."

"Is she pregnant?" Tobin asked with distaste. At least he was wise enough to use professionals, who knew better than to get pregnant.

"No, that's not it."

"Then what?"

"The sheriff and your son are both after the same girl."

"That waitress again." Tobin brought his hand down on his desk with a bang. "Why can't that boy just take himself a whore when the urge hits?"

Trehayne didn't have an answer to that. For himself, he thought a woman was a woman, whether he had to pay for her or not.

"All right, where is Dallas now?"

"He's out somewhere with Luke."

"Stirring up some trouble, no doubt. How many of our hands does my son count among his 'friends'?"

"I'd say about half a dozen."

"Can we afford to let them go?"

"Not now, but why bother at all? He'd just find himself another half dozen from the new men we hired. There's always somebody looking to get on the boss's son's good side."

"Simon, do you think that boy will ever make a good hand?"

"John, he's young—"

"Answer the question."

"No, I don't."

"What is he good for then?"

"Cut him loose and let him drift. He'd probably make a hell of a drifter."

"I can't do that."

Simon Trehayne looked at his long-time friend and said, "I know you can't."

"Find him for me, will you?"

"Sure."

"Send him over here, and then have a talk with his friends. Tell them anyone who starts trouble is out on his ass—and make that especially clear to Luke."

"It's a shame about Luke," Trehayne said.

"Why?"

"He does have the makings of a good hand, if it wasn't for Dallas's influence."

"Well, talk to him. See if you can smarten him up."

"All right."

"Simon."

"Yeah?"

"If Dallas gives you any lip, rough him up."

Trehayne hesitated, then said, "All right."

After Trehayne left to find Dallas, John Tobin got up from behind his desk to pour himself a drink. He considered the imported brandy, then decided on some good old American whiskey.

If the boy were anyone else but his own son, he'd have him whipped and thrown off the ranch.

In fact, maybe that wasn't such a bad idea after all, he thought. He wouldn't do it, but it wasn't a bad idea.

Chapter Fourteen

Clint and Bags left the hotel and went to have breakfast together.

"The café?" Clint asked.

"I don't think so."

"Why not?"

Bags looked at Clint, then said, "Yeah, why not?"

Trehayne went directly to the barn, where he knew Dallas would be holding forth. The foreman was a big, solid man—though not as large as Luke Joyner—and his mere presence commanded attention. As he entered the barn all conversation stopped.

"What can I do for you, Trehayne?" Dallas Tobin asked. He was seated on a bale of hay, with Luke Joyner sitting right behind him. The other six men were fanned out in front of them.

"Your father wants to see you, Dallas."

"In a while."

"Now."

Dallas looked directly at Trehayne and said, "I said I'd be along in a while."

Trehayne took a few steps into the barn and said, "Your father said now."

"You tell the old man I said in a while."

Trehayne came all the way into the barn and said, "Don't make this hard, boy."

Angry, Dallas stood up just as Trehayne reached him.

"You tell the old man—"

Trehayne's right hand came up and exploded against Dallas's right cheek in a backhanded blow that was hard enough to rattle his teeth.

Luke Joyner came to his feet and took a step toward Trehayne.

Though normally a soft-spoken man, when Trehayne spoke this time it was so loud that everyone in the barn was startled.

"You want to try me, boy?" he shouted, pointing his finger at the young giant. Trehayne, more than twenty years older than Joyner, almost hoped that the younger man *would* try him. It would be interesting.

Joyner, however, stopped cold at the sound of the foreman's voice.

"Anyone else?" Trehayne asked, looking at the six other men in the room. They all averted their eyes. "All right then." He put his hand on Dallas's shoulder and said, "Let's go to see your father, boy."

Dallas pulled away and rubbed his cheek with his hand. He turned and looked at Joyner, who was eyeing Trehayne with uncertainty, waiting for Dallas to give the word.

"Go ahead, Dallas," Trehayne said. "Tell him to go ahead."

"If I do, he'll take you apart."

"He'll try."

Dallas seemed to think about it, looking from Joyner to Trehayne and back.

"Nah," he said, "back off, Luke. You'd lose your job. We wouldn't want that, would we, Trehayne?"

"No, we wouldn't," the foreman said. "Unlike you, Luke's a good man to have around."

"We'd better go," Dallas said, "before I change my mind."

"The rest of you stay here," Trehayne said. "I'll be right back to talk to you."

Trehayne and Dallas left the barn and started walking to the house.

"You gonna go back and test my hold on them, Trehayne?"

The foreman didn't answer.

"They'll do whatever I say, you know."

"You don't pay them."

"Neither do you."

"I can fire them."

"I can have you fired. How do you like that, big man?" Dallas sneered.

Trehayne stopped. "You can have me fired?" Trehayne asked incredulously.

"One word from me to the old man and you're gone."

"Is that a fact?"

"Lay a hand on me again and find out."

"You got a deal."

Trehayne's right hand traveled a very short distance and slammed into Dallas Tobin's left side. Dallas's mouth opened and his eyes widened as he was suddenly unable to breathe. He fell to his knees, but Trehayne grabbed his arm and held him up.

"Let's go, sonny. Your daddy's waiting."

Dallas Tobin didn't say another word the rest of the way.

"Good morning, Nina," Joe Bags said as they entered.

Nina Katrina turned from the customer she was taking care of and stared at him in surprise. It was obvious that she had never expected to see him there again.

"Finish up there," Bags said. "We'll just take a table over here."

When they sat down Bags said, "Surprised, wasn't she?"

"I would say."

She came over and said, "What can I get you?"

"Eggs, ham, spuds, and a pot of coffee," Bags said, "for both of us."

"All right."

She stood there for a moment, as if she wanted to say something, then turned and went into the kitchen.

"What do I do next?"

"Ask her to have dinner with you?"

"Here?"

"Unless she can get someone to take her place while she goes somewhere else with you. She's got to have time off sometime, doesn't she?"

"Not if she runs the place herself."

"Suggest a picnic then."

"I don't know—"

"Go at your own pace, Joe. You could always wait until you take care of Dallas Tobin."

"Until *we* take care of the Tobins, Dallas and his papa."

"We meaning you and your deputies."

"Well, while you're here I figured you'd want to help—knowing you, I mean."

"Yeah, knowing me."

"Besides, you're after April, and you're not going to leave until you get her. Right?"

"Well, it's a challenge."

"What's wrong with you?" John Tobin asked his son.

Dallas had come into the room bent over, holding his side, and with a bruise on his face.

"That damn Trehayne," Dallas said, his face flooding angrily with blood. "I want him fired!"

"For what?"

"For what? He hit me . . . when I wasn't looking."

"I doubt that."

"Look at my face—"

"No, I don't doubt that he hit you, I just doubt that he did it while you weren't looking. He wouldn't have to do that—not with you."

"I said I want him fired."

"I don't give a good goddamn what you want. Sit down and shut up."

"But he hit me!"

"I told him to."

"You . . . what?"

"I told him that if you gave him any lip he was to rough you up. Knowing you, you couldn't help but try to tell him off, especially in front of your friends."

"He just works here—"

"Dallas, shut up!" John Tobin snapped.

Dallas Tobin shut up.

"Now, you and I are going to have a very serious talk."

"About what?"

"About the new sheriff, and your waitress girl-friend . . . ."

When Trehayne walked back into the barn conversation stopped again.

"I'm going to say this once. The first man who starts any trouble with the new sheriff is going to be out of a job. Understand?"

The six men looked at each other, and then one man spoke for all of them.

"Sure, boss."

"Just remember that," Trehayne said. "I'm the boss. Now get to work."

As the men started to file out Trehayne said, "Luke, you stay."

Joyner stopped and waited while the other six men left. When they were gone Trehayne faced Joyner squarely. The younger man was one of the few men Trehayne had had to look up to in his life.

"If I was you, I'd quit, take what pay I've got coming, and be on my way."

"Why?"

"Because you and me are gonna tangle, Luke, and you're gonna lose."

"Am I fired?"

"No, you're not fired."

"Then I better get to work."

"Stop following Dallas, Luke. He's gonna get you into a lot of trouble."

"He's my friend."

"Sure, he's your friend."

The big man left, and Trehayne followed him out, wondering how the meeting of the Tobins was going.

Chapter Fifteen

Clint and Bags were finishing off a second pot of coffee when the two new deputies, Kane and Jones, walked into the café and spotted them.

"Morning, Sheriff," Gimpy Kane called out.

Clint looked from Bags to Laramie Jones and wondered why the two men had taken an instant dislike to each other. Were they reacting like two studs vying for leadership of the herd?

Kane and Jones took their own table, and when Nina went over to take their order, it was plain that the handsome Laramie Kane was turning on the charm.

"That's what I need," Bags said.

Clint looked over and said, "More competition?"

"Yeah."

"I don't think so."

"Why?"

"He's not her type."

"What type is that?"

"Glib, good-looking, a fast talker."

"And what am I?"

"Attractive to some women, I guess, but more

honest, not as quick-tongued with a lie to a gal just to get her into your bed.''

"I guess I can't argue with that."

"Are you going to say anything to her before we leave?" Clint asked.

"I don't think so. Maybe . . . another time."

"Sure."

Nina came over after taking Kane's and Jones's orders and asked, "Can I get you anything else?"

"No," Clint said, "I think we've had enough. What do we owe you?"

She told them, and Clint stood up and paid her before Bags could.

"Sheriff," she said as they were leaving.

"Yes?"

"Could we . . . talk sometime? About yesterday?"

"What's to talk about?"

"I'd like to explain."

"Well . . . I'd like to listen, Nina."

"Could you come by tonight, after I close?"

"I'll be here."

"Thanks."

Bags turned and walked out. Clint moved to follow, then stopped and turned to Nina. "Nina."

"Yes?"

Indicating the two deputies, he said, "Make sure they pay for their breakfasts."

She grinned and said, "I will."

Outside, Clint clapped Bags on the back and said, "Well, that's a start."

After leaving his father, Dallas Tobin found Luke Joyner and pulled him aside.

"My old man is gonna try and buy the sheriff."

"Like he always does," Joyner said with a shrug.

"Well, I have a feeling this one is not gonna take the first offer."

"So?"

"That will give us time."

"To do what?"

"To take care of him."

"But Trehayne—"

"What did he have to say to you after I left?"

"That the first man who tried something with the sheriff would be out of a job."

"Don't worry about that. I'll take care of it."

"He also suggested I quit."

"Did he say why?"

Joyner nodded. "He said him and me was gonna tangle, and I was gonna lose."

"Do you believe that?"

"What?"

"That if you and Trehayne tangled, you'd lose?"

"He's an old man."

"That's right, he is. Look, you and the others just have to do what I say. As long as you do that, Trehayne can't fire you."

"Okay, Dallas."

"Tell the others, all right? We're going into town tonight."

"I'll tell them."

After Joyner went back to work, Dallas went into the barn to be alone. His father had warned him to stay away from the sheriff, and from Nina. Well, he wasn't about to heed that warning. The old man couldn't order him around like he did his foreman, and his hands.

Dallas Tobin was his own man, he told himself,

and he was going to show everyone.

"You know," Laramie Jones said to Gimpy Kane over their last cup of coffee, "this is one hell of a boring town."

"Didn't you find that cathouse last night?"

"I was playing poker."

"Then you must have lost."

"Just a little. I couldn't concentrate. All of the players kept staring at this tin star on my chest."

"Take it off then. Nobody says you have to wear it. Put it in your pocket."

"That's an idea."

Jones took the badge off his shirt and stuck it into his shirt pocket. "That feels better already. What did you do last night?"

"Me? *I* found the cathouse, and made liberal use of its wares."

"Had yourself a girl, huh?"

"Several."

"You're such a liar, Gimp."

"You know, don't you, that the only place I'm not gimpy is in bed?"

"Now how would I know a thing like that?"

"I'm telling you."

"And you're a notorious liar."

"That's no way to talk to your elders, whelp."

"Do you think you'd have a chance with her?" Jones asked, indicating the waitress.

"Her? She's too young for me. I like mature women."

"Well, she'd do fine for me," Jones said, watching Nina walk into the kitchen. "She'd do just fine."

"Maybe you'd better talk to the sheriff about that."

"The sheriff. Why?"

"You didn't see the way she was looking at him?"

"That waitress and the sheriff? You've got to be kidding."

"You and the sheriff haven't exactly hit it off, have you?"

"I don't think we'll ever be blood brothers."

"Well, he's your boss, so you better keep that in mind."

"He's not my boss," Jones said. "This deputy thing was your idea. You've got it in your head that you want to side with the Gunsmith. Well, Adams doesn't impress me any more than Bags does."

"You young whipper," Kane said. "You've got a lot of growing up to do if a man like Adams doesn't impress you."

"We'll see about that, Gimp," Jones said. "We'll just see."

A moment of silence passed between them, and then Laramie Jones said, "Yes, sir, this sure is a boring town."

"It'll liven up some," Gimpy Kane said with certainty. "It's got too much ingredients not to."

Chapter Sixteen

There was a knock on the office door, and when it opened, a solidly built man in his forties entered. Both Bags and Clint inspected him and decided that they would not ever want to have to trade punches with him.

"Sheriff?"

"I'm the sheriff," Bags said. It was unnecessary, since he was seated behind the desk and Clint was seated in front of it.

"My name is Trehayne, Sheriff," the man said, approaching the desk. "I'm the foreman on the Tobin ranch."

"I see," Bags said. "This is my friend, Clint Adams."

"Mr. Adams. Sheriff, I'd like to talk some business with you."

"What kind of business?"

Trehayne looked pointedly at Clint.

"Anything you want to say to me you can say in front of him."

"Did I misunderstand? Is he your deputy?"

"No, he's better than that. He's my friend."

"I see."

"What's on your mind, Mr. Trehayne?" Clint asked. "Or should I ask, What's on your employer's mind?"

Trehayne gave Clint a hard look, which Clint returned with a rather benign one.

"As a matter of fact, Mr. Tobin did send me," he said, and then directed his attention to Bags. "Whenever Rio Malo gets a new sheriff we make the same offer."

"What kind of an offer?"

"Mr. Tobin knows that a sheriff's salary is not very big. He usually offers to help supplement that salary."

"How much?" Clint asked.

Trehayne gave him an annoyed look, then pointedly ignored him and looked at Bags.

"How much?" Bags asked.

"Mr. Tobin feels that an additional one hundred dollars a month might help to make your job a little easier."

"Oh, it sure would. Wouldn't a hundred dollars a month make your job easier, Clint?"

"It sure would . . . and I don't even have a job, to speak of."

"And what would I have to do for this hundred dollars a month, Mr. Trehayne?"

Trehayne shrugged and said, "Well, Mr. Tobin feels that some sort of special consideration toward his men when they're in town might be in order."

"I see."

"Would that satisfy you?"

"Well, I don't know. I'll have to talk to my friend here." Bags looked at Clint and said, "Would that satisfy me?"

"Well, I don't know about you, but it sure wouldn't satisfy me—but then, he's not making the offer to me."

"Well, what would satisfy you then?"

"Well, two hundred dollars a month might satisfy me a little more."

"How about two hundred dollars?" Bags asked Trehayne.

"Well, two hundred—"

"Then again," Clint said, interrupting the foreman, "maybe it wouldn't. Maybe three hundred would be better."

"Maybe four?" Bags asked.

"Or four fifty . . ."

They both looked at Trehayne expectantly, and it didn't take the foreman long to figure out what was going on.

"You're making a mistake."

"No," Bags said, "your boss made the mistake."

"I'll tell him."

"And tell him to come himself with the next offer."

Trehayne gave Bags a hard look and said, "There won't be a second offer."

They both watched Trehayne leave. The room suddenly seemed much larger when he was gone.

"I guess I told him," Bags said.

"You sure did."

"He turned you down."

John Tobin regarded Trehayne silently, then asked, "How forceful were you?"

"Not very," Trehayne said, and then explained how Joe Bags and Clint Adams had played it.

"Apparently Adams has a great influence on Sheriff Bags. Can he be bought?"

In a tone of voice Tobin knew was deadly serious, Trehayne said, "I'd much rather kill him."

"Are you looking to add to your reputation, Simon?"

"It wouldn't hurt," Trehayne said, "but the simple fact of the matter is that I don't like the man."

"Well then, depending on how things go," Tobin said, "you might get your wish."

"There's only one problem," Clint said.

"What's that?"

"I knew a Trehayne once."

"He didn't seem to know you."

"I mean I knew *of* a Trehayne once, years ago."

"What about him."

"He was good."

"As good as you?"

"He dropped out of sight before anyone could find out how really good he was."

"So then you don't know how good he is?"

"I just said that."

Bags looked at the ceiling and said, "Great."

Chapter Seventeen

That night, when Dallas Tobin, Luke Joyner and their six compadres rode into town, Clint and Bags were once again sitting in the jail, playing two-handed poker.

Laramie Jones was in the Dancer House Saloon playing poker with four of the townspeople.

Gimpy Kane was standing at the bar in Rio Malo's smaller saloon, drinking slowly and watching the action.

As Kane had said earlier, all the ingredients were there.

"Where do we go?" Joyner asked as they dismounted.

"Well, let's stay away from Dancer's tonight. She's got her own gunhands."

"The other saloon then."

Dallas nodded and said, "The other saloon."

Clint took another hand from Joe Bags, who threw in his cards.

"We can't sit here all night playing cards. Why

don't we relieve Kane and Jones?''

"If they want to be relieved."

"If they don't, at least we can get a drink."

"Sounds good to me," Clint said, sliding his chair back and standing up. "I'll take Dancer's."

Bags grinned and said, "What a surprise."

Gimpy Kane noticed the men the moment they walked in. They came in three shifts, but the big one was the one who really attracted his attention. He was in company with a smaller man of the same age, and then behind them came three men, and then three more. He didn't know why they bothered to come in separately, because once inside they really made no effort to pretend that they didn't know each other. Such a pretense would have been useless in any case, because he assumed that they all worked for the same spread.

He'd been warned by Bags and Clint Adams to be on the lookout for trouble from men of the Tobin spread, and Dallas Tobin had been described to him. The smaller man in company with the large man fit the description.

Under normal circumstances a shotgun is an advisable weapon to have when facing a group of men —but the group must stay reasonably close together for the shotgun to be effective. In this case three men went to one side of the saloon, three to the other, and Dallas Tobin and his big friend found a poker table dead center. Tobin sat down to play, and Kane was sure he knew what the ploy was going to be.

It wasn't long in coming.

As soon as Dallas Tobin entered the saloon with

Luke Joyner he spotted the deputy at the bar. His instructions to his men had been to enter in threes behind him and Joyner, and then move to opposite ends of the saloon. He was pleased to see that this would be particularly effective because the deputy was carrying a shotgun.

Tobin found a poker game with an empty chair and took it. Joyner stood right behind him, arms folded.

It was just as Sheriff Joe Bags entered the saloon that Dallas Tobin—unaware of Bags's presence—made his move.

As Bags entered he saw Kane at the bar. Kane saw him and inclined his head to the center of the saloon. Bags found Dallas Tobin just as Tobin went into his act.

"Where did that ace come from?" he asked loudly.

Nothing stops the action in a saloon like an accusation of cheating at cards.

The man he was accusing was completely bewildered.

"What are you talking about? You were doing the dealing."

"That doesn't matter. I'm saying you're a cheater." Tobin looked past the player at the bartender. "Billy, you allow cheaters in your place?"

"He's a regular, Dallas," the man behind the bar said. "He don't cheat."

"If he's one of your regulars, Billy, then he must be working for you." Tobin looked behind him at Joyner and said, "You and the boys bust the place up, Luke."

"Right."

Joyner looked at the other six men and said, "Go."

"Hold it!" Bags shouted, pulling his gun. At the bar Kane shifted the shotgun from the crook of his arm to his hands.

"Well, well, our new sheriff," Dallas Tobin said. "You're looking at eight guns, Sheriff. You and your deputy. Why don't you go out and do some rounds, or something?"

"You're coming with me, Tobin."

"What for?"

"You're under arrest."

"For what?"

"Disturbing the peace."

"I haven't disturbed the peace yet."

"You're disturbing me."

Tobin shook his head and stood up. "I'm not going with you."

"Yes, you are."

"Luke, take the sheriff's gun."

"Sure."

As Joyner came around from behind Tobin, Bags saw that he wasn't wearing a gun.

"That's right, Sheriff. Luke doesn't wear a gun. He doesn't need one."

Bags could see why. Joyner was at least six-three, and solid. He couldn't very well shoot him, either, because he was unarmed.

Technically speaking.

"Get back, Luke."

"Luke only listens to me, Sheriff."

"I'm holding the gun."

"You won't use it. Not in front of all these people.

Luke's not armed," Tobin said, raising his voice so everyone could hear.

"Go ahead and shoot him," Kane said. "He'll take you apart."

"Damn!" Bags said, holstering his gun.

He moved to meet Joyner and swung first. He hoped he wouldn't have to justify that. His punch struck Joyner's jaw, but the man's head barely moved. He grinned and reached for Bags. The sheriff slid away from the big man's grasp and threw a punch into his midsection. His fist bounced off. It was like hitting the side of a barn.

Joyner swung a backhanded blow that caught Bags backing up. It glanced off his jaw, but his whole head seemed to vibrate from the force.

"Bags, use your gun!" Kane shouted.

"Can't . . ." Bags said, circling the big man.

I wish I could, he thought . . . .

Clint was watching Laramie Jones play poker when a man poked his head into the saloon.

"Sheriff's got trouble over at Billy's. He's fighting Luke Joyner."

Several people started for the door, wanting to see that, but Clint moved first, blocking the door.

"Everybody stay put. First man I see poke his head into the other saloon is under arrest." It didn't occur to anyone in the place that Clint Adams was not a deputy. The tone of his voice said he was in charge.

"Laramie!"

Jones glanced sorrowfully at the full house in his hand, then threw the cards down and shouted, "On my way!"

•　　•　　•

Joyner lunged, grabbed Bags by the shirt and lifted him up bodily. He moved his other hand to Bags's crotch and lifted him over his head. Everyone scattered because they didn't know where Joyner was going to throw him.

"Put him down!" Kane shouted, pointing his shotgun at Joyner. "Tell him to put the sheriff down, Tobin. Maybe he wouldn't shoot an unarmed man, but I sure as hell would."

Tobin knew that Kane was telling the truth.

"Kill him!" Dallas Tobin shouted at his six men.

All six of them drew their guns, and the rest of the patrons in the saloon either ran for cover or dropped to the floor.

Kane picked out the three he would take with him and fired both barrels. The double-o buckshot leaped across the room, its pattern widening, and slammed into the three men.

Clint Adams came barreling through the bat-wing doors, followed closely by Laramie Jones, both with their guns drawn. They spotted the other three men about to fire on Kane and opened fire on them. As the three men went down, two of them managed to get off a shot. One went wild and struck a whiskey bottle on a shelf behind the bar. The other one struck Kane in the left shoulder, slamming him back against the bar.

That left Dallas Tobin and the big man, Luke Joyner.

"Hey, can we get me down from here?" Joe Bags asked. Joyner, holding the sheriff over his head, did not seem to be straining at all. He was watching Dallas Tobin curiously, waiting for instructions.

Clint and Laramie Jones both pointed their guns at Luke Joyner, and Clint said, "Put him down real easy."

Dallas Tobin went for his gun, but Clint saw him and moved the barrel of his gun away from the big man to cover Tobin and keep him from firing at them. What he didn't expect, however, was that Tobin would fire at the man he had accused of cheating.

"Tobin!" Clint shouted after the man had fired once.

Tobin's gun was still pointing at the fallen man as he turned his head to look at Clint.

"Give me an excuse, Tobin."

"Take it easy," Tobin said, pulling his hand away from his gun. "All I did was kill a card cheat."

"Drop the gun, Tobin."

Tobin obeyed and said, "Besides, we were just having some fun before you busted in here."

"Well, your fun got six of your friends killed, and the big boy here is going to join them if he doesn't put the sheriff down."

Tobin seemed to be trying to make up his mind, but finally said, "Put him down, Luke."

Joyner set Bags down on his feet easily and released him. Bags took out his gun and slammed Joyner across the jaw with it. The big man staggered back a couple of steps and then shook his head, blood leaking from a tear in his cheek, but he never went down.

"Jesus," Bags said. "Let's get these polecats over to the jail."

"You can't put me in jail," Dallas Tobin said.

"Just watch me," Bags said.

Clint moved to Tobin's side, removed his gun, and pushed him toward the door.

Laramie Jones went to Kane, who was slumped against the bar, bleeding from the shoulder.

"Gimp?"

"I'm fine."

"Get him to the doctor," Clint told Jones.

"Get my shotgun."

Jones picked it up off the floor and then grabbed hold of Kane's elbow. "Let's go get that bullet taken out."

"Wait a minute. Take me over there."

Jones took Kane over to where the three men he'd shot were lying. Two of them were obviously dead, while the third was writhing on the floor, buckshot having nearly torn his arm off.

"Shit," Kane said. They should have all died instantly. "I'm losing my touch."

Helping his partner from the saloon, Jones said, "You know, I had to throw in a full house to come and help you."

"Excuse me if I don't apologize."

Also present in the saloon at the time of the shooting was Bob Richardson. Although a hand on the Tobin ranch, Richardson didn't have much use for John Tobin's son. He did, however, have loyalty to his boss, and felt compelled to ride out to give him the bad news of his son's apparent arrest.

Richardson got up off the floor and watched the sheriff and his men march Dallas Tobin out of the saloon, then he rushed out, mounted his horse, and rode for the Tobin ranch.

Chapter Eighteen

Bags came out from the back and tossed the cell keys on the desk. "We've got trouble now," he said.

"What do you mean?"

Pointing to the cells in the back, Bags said, "I've got John Tobin's son in a cell."

"Come on, Bags," Clint said. "Before you came here you didn't even know who John Tobin was."

"Well, I know now," Bags said, sitting down. "He's going to come storming in here to get his son, and all I've got to stand against him is a poker player, a gimp with a bullet in his shoulder, and you."

"Thanks a lot."

"You know what I mean. Tobin's got I don't know how many hands on his spread. If he wanted to he could tear this jail down around us to get his son out."

"I think you're putting the cart before the horse here, Bags."

"What does that mean?"

"I don't think that Tobin's first reaction is going to be to come tearing into town with all his men. He'll probably come in and talk to you."

"About what? Bailing his son out? The kid committed murder, for Chrissake, right in front of a saloon full of witnesses! I'm the only one who didn't see it, because that big jerk was holding me the wrong way!"

"He'll come in and talk to you first, and see if he can buy you."

"Trehayne tried that, remember? We put him on and he got mad. He said there wouldn't be another offer."

"That was before you had his son in jail for murder."

"I've had this job a week and already I've got the son of the biggest man in town in my jail."

"Maybe you should have taken him up on his offer."

Bags looked at Clint, then said, "No, I did the right thing."

"Everything you've done up to now has been right, Bags," Clint said. "Just don't back off now."

Bags looked at Clint and said, "Tough job, huh?"

"Not too tough for you."

"I guess we'll see about that, huh?"

"Take my word for it."

"So what's our next move?"

"You'll have to send for a judge, and just hold the fort until he gets here."

"With just three deputies, huh?"

"Two deputies and a friend," Clint corrected him. "Besides, that's twice as many deputies as you had when you took the job."

"Well, I guess we'd better check and see how Kane is, and then see what they have to say about it."

Clint grinned and said, "Good thinking, Sheriff."

When they got to the doctor's office Laramie Jones was helping Gimpy Kane on with his shirt. Clint and Bags saw that Kane's chest was a map of scars, but neither said anything. His face was a map of bumps and wrinkles, and they hadn't asked about that either. Obviously the man had lived a full if somewhat hard life.

"How you doing, Gimpy?" Clint asked.

"I'm fine. The doc got the bullet out, and I'm ready to go back to work."

"That's what we want to talk to you about . . . both of you," Bags said.

When the doctor came out, Bags settled up with him because Kane had been wounded while working. After that they all went back to the office, which shouldn't have been left untended with prisoners in the cell.

"All right, what is it you want to talk to us about?" Kane asked, grimacing as he sat down.

"You know who we've got in a cell back there, and you know why."

"Dallas Tobin," Kane said.

"For murder, I hope," Laramie Jones said.

"Right on both counts," Bags said. He then launched into a big explanation of what he thought was going to happen next. They were going to have to hold Dallas Tobin until a judge arrived. There was no doubt but that his father was going to try and get him out.

"Clint feels he'll try to buy his way out first."

"I bet he'd pay a lot too," Jones said.

"He probably would, but I'm not selling," Bags said.

"I never said you would."

"When I turn him down there could be some fireworks. I want you two to know that I won't hold you to your oaths."

"I hope you won't try," Kane said, "because you forgot to give them to us."

"Oh. Well, even if I had, I wouldn't hold you to them. You're free to ride on."

"Well, I'll tell you," Kane said, shifting in his seat in search of comfort, "I took a bullet and killed three men to put young Mr. Tobin where he is right now. I'd kind of like to take a hand in putting him where he belongs for good."

Bags looked at Laramie Jones and said, "How about you, Jones?"

Jones shrugged and said, "I don't have anything better to do. Is Adams staying?"

"I'm staying, at least until the judge shows up," Clint replied.

"As a deputy?" Jones asked.

"As an interested and active party."

"Well, I guess what my partner said to me earlier in the day was right."

"What did he say?" Clint asked.

"Yeah, what did I say?"

"That it was bound to get interesting around here."

All four men exchanged glances, and then Clint said, "Well, it certainly has done that."

Chapter Nineteen

When Bob Richardson reached the Tobin spread with the news, the first man he gave it to was Simon Trehayne.

"Is he under arrest?"

"Mr. Trehayne, he shot that man stone cold dead in front of everyone, including the sheriff. You're damn right he's under arrest."

Trehayne's initial reaction was that he was glad. This would get the boy out of John Tobin's hair for good. He came to his senses almost immediately, however, realizing that John Tobin would never let his son go to jail, no matter how much he may have deserved it.

"All right, Richardson. You'd better turn in. I'll give Mr. Tobin the news."

"Thanks, Boss. I didn't fancy doing that myself."

Trehayne didn't much fancy doing it himself either.

When Clint returned to his hotel that evening he found a message waiting for him at the desk.

It was from April Dancer.

He read it right there, then folded it, put it in his pocket, and left. The gist of the message summed up what he had been feeling the previous night, when he'd rejected her offer. He'd been mistaken, he thought, not to take her to bed then.

He wasn't going to make that mistake again.

Joe Bags left Laramie Jones at the sheriff's office, after Jones had taken Kane back to their hotel room to get some rest. Bags knew that Nina Katrina lived above the café, and that's where he went now.

They'd had an appointment which he had been unable to keep.

It was time to keep it.

John Tobin did not take the news well.

"Goddamn that boy!" he shouted. He'd been sitting, and now he stood and pounded the desk with his fist. "Damn him!"

Simon Trehayne stood silently, waiting for his employer and friend to ask a question.

Tobin fumed and glared at the ceiling, then fixed his gaze on Trehayne. "Did he do it?"

"Oh, yes."

"Witnesses?"

"A whole saloon full."

"What the hell was he thinking!"

"You'll excuse me for saying so, John, but I think he figured you could buy him out of anything."

"Well, I can't buy him out of this," John Tobin said. "We'll have to get him out another way."

"We should make an offer," Trehayne said.

"Do you think Bags would take it?"

"No."

"Then why make the offer?"

"I would just rather try everything within the law before going outside it."

"Bribing a sheriff to let him go is within the law?"

"It's a lot closer than breaking him out."

"Who said anything about breaking him out?"

"You said we'd have to find another way," Trehayne reminded him. "What other way could there be?"

Tobin didn't have an answer for that.

The note told Clint to use the side entrance. When he knocked, the door was immediately opened by April Dancer.

"Come in."

"I got your note," he said, holding it up in front of him.

"Obviously," she said, taking it from him.

"It seems . . . suggestive."

"It was," she said. She shrugged her shoulders and her nightgown fell in a heap around her ankles.

Her breasts were breathtaking, large and firm, with distended brown nipples. She was in her bare feet and still almost stood eye to eye with him. The heat from her body was intense.

"So is this."

"Yes," he agreed, "it certainly is."

"I don't want anything for this. No special considerations. I just want . . . this," she said, reaching out for him.

"So do I."

He took her into his arms and kissed her, a kiss

that was immediately deep and intense.

Moments later they were on her bed, naked, searching with their hands and mouths, tasting each other, learning each other's bodies even before they would learn anything else about each other . . . .

When Nina Katrina opened her door, Joe Bags grabbed her and kissed her. She resisted momentarily, then melted against him and returned the kiss with vigor.

"Bastard," she said when he released her.

"You're finished with Dallas Tobin."

Breathing hard, she simply said, "Yes," and then they were kissing again . . .

. . . and then they were on her bed and he was deep inside her, holding her buttocks tightly, driving in and out of her again and again while she called his name. . . .

John Tobin finally calmed down enough to sit back down behind his desk. Trehayne waited, hoping that any decision his old friend made would be rational.

"All right, Simon, go and turn in for the night. Meet me here in the morning."

"I'm . . . sorry about this, John."

"I know, Simon, I know. I appreciate that. In the morning we'll ride into town and try whatever legal means we can to get Dallas released."

"And failing that?"

Tobin pinned Trehayne with a hard stare and said, "We'll get him out, Simon, one way or another. We'll get him out."

• • •

Clint woke the next morning in April Dancer's bed. The night had been a memorable one, and when he saw her lying on her back, naked, he felt himself rising and knew that the night was not quite over yet.

Happily . . .

Sheriff Joe Bags woke with Nina Katrina's head between his legs. Her tongue was eager, darting up and down until he was fully erect, and suddenly she engulfed him eagerly and ravenously drained him.

Later she said, "Come downstairs and I'll fix you breakfast before I open."

"What about you?"

She grinned, licked her lips and said, "I've already had breakfast."

"What happens now?" Clint asked as he dressed.

April looked at him from the bed. She was still naked, but she had the sheet drawn over her. It molded itself to every dip and rise in her body.

"Nothing, Clint. I was attracted to you and I did something about it. It can happen again, or not. I guess that would be your choice."

"April—"

"I just want you to know I meant what I said last night," she said, interrupting him before he could go on. "There are no conditions."

"You don't want me to help you get out from under John Tobin's influence?"

"Yes, I do," she said, "but I want you to *want* to help me—and not because I bribed you."

He sat down on the bed and put his hand on her

knee. "Money's a bribe, April," he said, "sex is a favor."

"Well, if that's the case," she said, "would you do me a favor before you leave?"

He got undressed again. . . .

Chapter Twenty

Clint and Bags met at the sheriff's office, each feeling a sense of great satisfaction, and each having had a breakfast fit for more than mere mortal men.

Laramie Jones was sitting at the desk with his head down on his arms, seemingly fast asleep.

"Come on, Laramie," Clint said, nudging him awake.

Jones looked up calmly at the two of them, then sat up. He was remarkably clear-eyed for a man who had been asleep moments before.

"Why didn't you sack out in an empty cell?" Bags asked him.

"I tried that. The kid kept me up by telling me what his father was going to do to us for putting him in jail."

"Forget that," Bags said. "Go and get some sleep and check on Kane. If he's not well enough, tell him to stay in his room today."

"Oh, he'll be well enough to come out," Jones said, standing up. "I could use the sleep though. We'll be over here in a few hours, if that's okay."

"Fine."

Jones nodded and left.

"He's not so bad after all," Bags said.

"I guess not."

"What are our plans for the day?"

"You're the sheriff, but I'd say we send a wire for a judge and then wait for John Tobin to make a move."

"Sounds good to me."

"Hey!" they heard a voice call from the cell.

"Shut up, Tobin!" Bags shouted. "I don't want to hear about what your father is going to do to me."

"We want some breakfast!"

"Hungry, are you?" Bags asked, sticking his head into the back so he could see them.

"I'm starving," Luke Joyner said.

"You would be," Bags said. "Sit still and keep quiet, and I'll see what I can do."

In truth, he had already arranged with Nina to send breakfast over for the prisoners. He just had to wait for her to find someone to bring it.

"I'm going to send the wire, Clint. Will you stay here with these two?"

"Sure. Hey, what happened to you last night?"

"What do you mean?"

"You look relaxed."

"I am relaxed."

"What happened?"

"The same thing that happened to you, I'll wager. You look pretty relaxed, yourself."

"Funny," Clint said, "I didn't see you there."

John Tobin refused Simon Trehayne's suggestion that they take more men to town with them.

"I'm not interested in a show of force at this time," Tobin said. "That will come later."

"We'll be outnumbered—"

"We're only going into town to talk, Simon," Tobin reminded his foreman. "Besides, you're wearing your gun, aren't you?"

"Yes."

"Then we're not so outnumbered," Tobin said with confidence.

Bags was coming out of the telegraph office when he spotted the two men riding down the center of the street. Both sat tall in the saddle, their animals moving forward with purposeful strides. It was as if they knew that anyone who was in their way would immediately move aside.

And they did.

Bags recognized Simon Trehayne immediately, and assumed that the other man was John Tobin.

They rode toward his office, and he knew they would get there before him.

Clint was seated at Bags's desk when the door opened and Simon Trehayne walked in, in the company of another, older man he'd assumed was John Tobin. Tobin was as tall as Trehayne, but much slimmer. Still, on his own he was not an unimpressive figure.

"Is that him?" the man asked.

"That's Adams," Trehayne said.

"What's a man like you doing here in Rio Malo, Adams? Has somebody hired your gun?"

"I assume you're John Tobin."

"I asked you a question."

Clint remained silent.

"I'm Tobin," John Tobin finally admitted. "What are you doing here?"

"Just visiting an old friend."

"You just happened to be here, huh?"

"That's right. What are you doing here?"

Tobin glared at Clint, then said, "I want to see my son."

"I can't let you do that, Tobin."

"Why not?"

"I'm not a deputy, and the sheriff's not here. You'll have to wait until he returns."

"Why are you here in the office then?"

Clint shrugged. "I'm just minding the store. You may have heard, a deputy was injured last night."

"And when will the sheriff be back?"

"Any moment now. He's sending a wire."

"A wire?"

"For a judge. Your son will have to stand trial for murder."

Tobin's jaw clenched, and he said, "I thought you said you weren't a deputy?"

"I'm not."

"Then I'd appreciate you keeping your opinions to yourself."

"Fine."

"I want to see my son."

"This isn't an opinion," Clint prefaced. "I can't let you see him."

Tobin seemed about to lash out angrily when he caught himself and changed his tact. "Adams, it could be worth a lot of money to you to help me on this."

"How much money?"

Again Tobin seemed about to speak and stopped. This time he remembered what Trehayne said Clint and Bags had done to him, putting him on about money.

Trehayne started to come forward when the door opened and Sheriff Bags stepped in.

"Company, Clint?"

"You know Mr. Trehayne, Sheriff. This gentleman is John Tobin, Dallas's father."

"Well," Bags said, "I suppose you'll want to see your son."

"In a moment," Tobin said. "First I want to talk to you."

"Oh?" Bags said. He came over to the desk to change places with Clint, who gave him a stern look that clearly stated, Stand your ground.

"What do you want to talk to me about?" Bags asked, seating himself behind his desk.

"Bail."

"No bail."

"What do you mean?"

"I mean I can't give your son bail. He killed a man in cold blood in front of a roomful of witnesses. If I let him out, he'll be gone."

"You can release him in my custody."

"Can't," Bags said, shaking his head. "You'd send him away first thing."

"How dare you—"

"I dare, Mr. Tobin. I'm the law here, and I say your son stays where he is until a judge gets to town."

"And how long is that?"

"Can't tell. Days, a week—"

"Don't make me send some wires of my own, Sheriff. I am not without influence."

"You go ahead and influence whoever you want by wire, but you're not influencing me, Mr. Tobin, and I'm right here."

"I want my son released, Sheriff."

"Wanting ain't getting, Tobin, and it never has been, so you go on wanting all you want. That boy of yours will sit in my jail until the judge gets here."

"We'll see about that."

"Yes, we will." ·

Tobin glared at Bags murderously, graced Clint with a piece of the same look, then turned and headed for the door, Trehayne right behind him.

As Tobin was leaving, Bags called out, "You should have taught the boy better, Mr. Tobin."

Tobin turned, gave Bags a mournful look, and said, "I can't argue that with you."

They left, and as Trehayne walked out behind him, Clint was almost sure that the foreman could fit right in Tobin's pocket with no trouble at all. He was sorry to have to feel that way. What little memory he had of Simon Trehayne's reputation was good. He wondered what had turned him into John Tobin's yes man.

"I saw them coming when I was at the telegraph office, knew I couldn't beat them here."

"That's okay," Clint said. "We just got acquainted while we waited for you. We had a nice little conversation about . . . things."

"Anything I should know?"

"Well, for one thing, he tried to buy me."

"For how much?"

"Uh, for a lot, he said."

"How much?"

"We never got around to amounts," Clint said, a bit sheepishly.

"You never got around to it? It must be nice to have that much money that you even forgot to ask."

"I got something better than money."

"What's that?"

"Integrity."

"I'm glad you didn't say brains. What did you think of Papa Tobin?"

"I think I know where his son gets it."

"Gets what?"

"Thinking that his father's money can buy him out of anything. In the pinch his father fell back on offering me money. It's the only way they know how to live."

"If it was the only way, we wouldn't have anything to worry about."

"You're right about that."

"You know what?" Joe Bags said.

"What?"

"He left without seeing his son."

"You know what?"

"What?"

"I don't think he ever really wanted to."

"Why?"

"If your son got you into a predicament like this, what would you do to him?"

"I'd kill him."

"And he's got enough problems as it is, don't you think?"

Chapter Twenty-One

An hour later they were all gathered in the office for a meeting. Bags had gone over everything first with Clint, who had simply listened to his plans and agreed with them. He might have been able to make a refinement or two, but he thought it best to let the new sheriff make his own plans.

Bags was behind his desk and Clint was standing by the potbellied stove, waiting for the coffee to be ready. Laramie Jones and Gimpy Kane were sitting in the two chairs in front of Bags's desk.

"Tobin's father was in today," Bags began. "He tried money and he tried threats to get his son out of jail. Neither one worked."

"Well, we all know what comes after that," Laramie Jones said.

"Force," Kane added.

"Right. This is how I'd like to work it. One of us has got to be in here at all times—and I mean all the time. No going out for something to eat."

"Which one of us?" Kane asked.

"We'll take turns."

"I have a suggestion."

"I'm listening."

"I don't get around so good on this leg," Kane said, "and now this shoulder is gonna slow me down even more. Why don't I just bunk in here until the judge comes? You fellas can take turns coming in to keep me company. That way we'll have two people in here at all times."

Bags looked at Clint, then at Jones. Both of them seemed to approve.

"That's fine. Laramie, you mind bringing his gear over for him?"

"I'll do it as soon as we're finished here."

"Okay, good. The next thing we have to deal with is weapons. This office is not well stocked with guns. In fact there are none, as you can see by the empty racks."

"I don't think that's a problem, Joe," Clint said. "We've all got our own guns."

"Everybody satisfied with that?"

Both Kane and Jones nodded.

"Okay. The two who are out will be responsible for bringing meals in to the two who are in. This way both of the inside men can stay inside."

Everyone agreed.

"Also, the outside men will bring meals in for the prisoners."

Again they were all in agreement.

The coffee was ready at that point, and Clint handed out cups.

"Anybody got any questions?"

"How long before the judge gets here?" Jones asked.

Bags looked uncomfortable. "I haven't had a reply yet from my wire."

"So we don't know yet if we're even going to get a judge, let alone when."

"I should have a reply later today."

"You hope."

"What about the big kid?" Kane asked.

"What about him?"

"Well, he didn't fire a shot. What are we holding him for?"

"For assaulting me."

"Couldn't we let him out on bail? It would give us one less to worry about in here."

"And one more to worry about outside," Clint said.

"Good point," Bags said. "Besides, Tobin never said anything about bailing Joyner out. In fact he never even mentioned him to me."

"Or me."

"I guess he's only concerned with his son," Laramie Jones said.

"Right."

"Okay, anyone else got anything to say?" Bags asked.

"I do," Clint said. "At one time or another two of us are going to be cooped up together here. I think a bath wouldn't be a bad idea."

"For who?" Kane demanded.

Kane, obviously the scruffiest of the four, felt everyone's eyes on him.

"All of us," Clint said.

"Nobody said anything about a bath when I hired on," Kane complained.

"There's a metal tub in the back," Bags said. "Somebody would just have to supply the water."

"I will," Jones said, grinning.

"Traitor!"

"I've been trying to get him to take a bath for days and days."

"Okay, if there's nothing else, then, we're all set."

"Not quite," Jones said. "How far are we going to go to keep these boys in jail?"

"What do you mean, how far?" Bags asked.

"I think he means will we be killing anybody to prevent his being busted out?"

"We'll do what has to be done," Bags said. "Whatever has to be done."

"Is that clear enough?" Clint asked.

"It's clear," Jones said, standing up. "I'll collect Gimp's things and bring them right over, and then I'll get the water."

"I'll help you," Clint offered.

"It's great to have so many friends who care about you," Kane said glumly.

"It's not you we're looking out for, old buddy," Laramie Jones said, slapping the older man on the back. "It's us."

Chapter Twenty-Two

When John Tobin returned home he wanted to do some thinking. For that he needed to relax, and for that he needed a whore. He had left Trehayne behind in Rio Malo to arrange that, and he would be along any moment. A good long session with one of Jenny Lee's girls would relax him enough for him to think straight.

When Trehayne arrived, Tobin was waiting in his bedroom. Trehayne knocked, opened the door, ushered the girl in and backed out, closing the door.

"Hello, Mr. Tobin."

Her name was Mary—or Marion, something like that—and she was one of his favorites. She was young, blond, full-breasted, and talented at what she did.

He opened his robe and discarded it. His penis was semi-erect, but she knew what he wanted. She undressed and knelt before him. First she rolled his penis between her big breasts, and when it started to get stiffer, she leaned forward and took it into her mouth.

He closed his eyes, cupped the back of her head, and moaned as she started sucking him. Soon his legs began to tremble, and then he cried out, filling her mouth. She cupped his buttocks and managed to take his full load without losing a drop.

Talented, he thought, real talented.

"I may not be able to come up here for a while," Clint said to April Dancer.

"Why not?"

"With Tobin's son in a cell, Joe Bags is going to need all the help he can get."

"He's got deputies, hasn't he?"

"They're just his deputies," Clint said, "and I'm his friend."

They were lying naked on her bed in her room above the saloon. They had just finished making love, slowly and intensely, and were now resting with their limbs still entwined. There was a cool breeze from the window, which was open a crack, and the perspiration covering their bodies was cooling.

"Well," she said, "if this is going to be the last time for a while, we might as well make the most of it."

"That's why I'm here. . . ."

At the same time, in Nina Katrina's room, Joe Bags and Nina were in a similar situation, discussing the same thing.

"We can still see each other," Nina Katrina said to Joe Bags.

"Honey, I'd like nothing better—"

"I'll bring your meals to the jail."

"No, one of us will pick up the meals every day. I don't want you near the jail."

"Joe," she said, rolling over so that she could put

her head on his chest and press her breasts against his side.

"It'll be all right, honey."

"Why don't you just give up the badge?" she asked. "You could get work around town."

"I worked a long time for this badge, Nina. I'm not going to give it up that easily—especially not because of any threats from a man like John Tobin."

"You're stubborn."

"Yes," he said, "and I'm ready."

The sheet was covering his groin, but she could see that he was indeed ready. She leaned down so she could move the sheet down and take him in her mouth. . . .

Simon Trehayne stood outside the Tobin ranch house, looking up at Tobin's window. When had he come to this? he wondered—supplying women for John Tobin. He had done a lot for Tobin over the years, and he was willing to do a lot more—but when Tobin said something like, "Get me a whore," it made him wonder if he still wanted to work for the same man.

Or even be his friend.

Maybe, he thought, I ought to go and get myself a whore.

Or a sheriff.

"How do you feel?" Laramie Jones asked Gimpy Kane.

"Strange."

"That's the way you look."

Indeed, Gimpy Kane clean was a sight to behold. They were in the sheriff's office, and Kane had just dressed after his bath. All he'd need was a shave and no one would be able to recognize him, Jones thought, not even his own mother. If he ever had one.

"You sure smell good."

"Where the hell did you get that soap?" Kane complained, sniffing himself. "I smell like a two-dollar whore."

"That's where I got it from," Jones said. "I made myself a friend over at Jenny Lee's whorehouse."

"Jesus, you couldn't find another kind of soap?"

Laramie Jones smiled and said, "I don't know. I didn't try."

Clint left April's room at the same time Bags left Nina's. They had agreed to meet in April's saloon for a drink before heading for the office.

Clint was coming down the side stairway when he heard the shots. He ran out into the street and listened for further shots, hoping to use them to pinpoint the location. He was rewarded with two more shots, and then a third, and decided that they were coming from the direction of Nina's café.

Where Joe Bags was.

He started to run toward the café, which was a few blocks away. As with April Dancer's room, there was access from the outside, as well as from the café and he saw the three men standing at the mouth. Two of them fired into the darkness, and the third spotted Clint and shouted something to the others.

A couple of shots came from within the alley, and then the three men turned and fired at Clint. He hit the ground rolling and came up with his gun out, but the three men were already running away. The odds had become much too even for them. Clint knew it was useless to fire after them in the darkness and holstered his gun.

He walked to the mouth of the alley, careful not to let himself be seen. He didn't want to get himself shot by a friend by accident.

"Bags!" he shouted. "Bags, it's Clint."

"Clint?"

"You can come out."

In a moment Bags appeared from the dark recesses of the alley, gun in hand. His hat was off and Clint could see how high his forehead had become. Funny that he'd notice that now, of all times.

From the darkness behind him also came Nina Katrina, looking worried.

"Are you all right?" Clint asked.

"Yeah, I'm fine," Bags said, holstering his gun. "Let me get Nina back upstairs and find my hat and I'll be right out."

Waiting for Bags, Clint assumed that Nina had heard the shots and come rushing out. Bags would now be trying to placate her and assure her that he was all right.

When he appeared again, Clint asked, "You sure you're okay?"

"They were too overanxious and fired too fast, or they would have had me."

"Did you see who they were?"

"No, not from in there. Did you?"

"No. They started firing and I had to scramble. I could probably guess though."

"So could I."

"I think we should change our plans, Bags."

"Because of this?"

"Yes."

"How?"

"If they're going to try and pick us off one at a time, maybe we should all just hole up in the jail until the judge gets here."

"Think we could stand each other?"

"As long as we keep each other alive, we can stand each other. Come on, we'll collect some gear and then let Laramie and Gimp do the same."

"Laramie already collected Gimpy's things."

"All right, we'll let Laramie get his things, we'll stock up on cards, and have a week-long poker game. . . ."

"Or month long . . ." Bags said.

Or longer . . .

From the window of a room in Jenny Lee's whorehouse, which overlooked the main street, Simon Trehayne could see Clint Adams and Sheriff Joe Bags walking past. That meant his men had failed in their attempt to waylay the sheriff.

"Simon? Come back to bed. I'm cold."

He turned and looked at the woman on the bed. She was tall and slender, with small breasts that fit his hands perfectly, and his mouth. Her name was Stefanie, and he found himself oddly excited by the fact that she had almost as much dark black hair between her legs as she did on her head.

Sending the three men after Bags had been an afterthought. His main reason for coming to town was to see Stefanie. He turned away from the window, his erection huge and prodding at the air.

"You won't be cold for long, Steffie."

As he approached the bed she reached for him eagerly. Even though she was a whore, she was impressed with the size of his manhood, and she usually spent a lot of time working over it before they got down to serious business.

To hell with Bags, John Tobin, and Clint Adams.

Chapter Twenty-Three

The office was filled with smoke, most of it coming from Gimpy Kane's cigar. Laramie Jones rolled an occasional cigarette and added to the haze.

This had been home for these four men for two days now, and that was how long the poker game had been going on. When two of them left the office to get food, the other two continued the game two-handed. Kane was spared running errands because of his wound and his bad leg, so he was always at the poker table with at least one of the others. He was also the only man who was ahead in the game.

Clint had dealt this hand and was sitting with a pair of Queens in a Jacks-or-better-to-open game of draw poker.

"I pass," Bags said.

"Me too," Laramie Jones said.

"I open," Kane said with a grin.

"You have a terrible poker face, Gimp," Laramie Jones said sourly. He considered himself the best player in the game and was miffed that he was losing.

"I know."

"I call," Clint said.

"I'm out," Bags said. He wasn't a poker player

and was just in the game to pass the time. So far, passing the time had cost him twenty dollars, because he played conservatively and dropped out when the stakes got too high. Like now.

Jones called, and Clint replaced each man's discards.

Jones took three. He played a straightforward game and hardly ever bluffed. He was sitting with a low pair, hoping to improve.

"I'll play these," Kane said.

"You're full of shit," Jones said.

Technically, Clint could see that Jones was a better player than Kane. The difference, however, was that Kane didn't care if he won or lost, and Jones desperately wanted to win to prove he was the better player.

Clint took three cards, looked at them, and couldn't believe his eyes. His face betrayed nothing.

"Opener," he said.

"I bet ten dollars," Kane said.

Clint made a show of studying his cards, and also studied the faces of the men around the table. If he raised, he might scare the other two players out. Then again, the fact that Kane had stood pat with his hand might scare them out anyway. If Clint didn't raise now, he might never get the chance.

"I raise, twenty dollars."

"Shit," Jones said. He studied Clint's face, then Kane's. "He's bluffing," he said, indicating Kane, then said to Clint, "You took three cards, but I don't know what the hell you're up to."

"That's why it's called gambling," Clint said. "Call or fold . . . unless you want to raise."

"I'll call."

Bags was already out and was up, getting himself a

cup of coffee. He came back with it to watch the outcome.

Kane regarded Clint for a while, then checked his hand. That was when Clint knew he had him. He didn't think the man was bluffing, but he was in doubt about the strength of his hand, in spite of the fact that he'd stood pat.

"I call."

Clint showed his hand, all four Queens.

"Damn!" Jones said, throwing his cards down.

"Get dealt a flush and lose the hand," Kane said, putting his cards down face up to reveal an Ace high heart flush. "Guess my luck must be changing."

"I guess," Clint said, raking in his money.

"Come on, Laramie," Bags said, dropping a hand onto the man's shoulder. "Let's make a meal run."

"Might as well, I'm not having any luck here."

"We'll play on," Kane said, unnecessarily, after Bags and Laramie left. He picked up the cards and began to straighten them out.

Usually when two of the men were away, the other two got to know each other a little better.

"Want to know about my leg?" Kane asked.

"What makes you ask that?"

Kane shrugged. "Got to talk about something, don't we? I figure instead of waiting for you to figure out how to bring it up, I might as well do it myself."

"All right then," Clint said as Kane dealt out a hand of five-card stud, "what happened to your leg?"

"Got bayoneted during the war."

"Bayoneted?"

"Yep. I ain't saying what side I was on, but I come face to face with somebody from the other side one day. We both raised our rifles to fire, and damned if we wasn't both out of ammunition."

"What happened then?"

"Your King bets."

Clint bet a dollar. Kane called and dealt out the next card.

"What happened then?" Clint asked.

"Well, we both went for each other with our bayonets. I caught him right through the gut, and his bayonet tore open my thigh. It was a damned deep tear, too, bled like a bastard. I walked a long way before I found my way to a field hospital."

"What did the doctor say?"

"King still bets."

That wasn't what the doctor said, and Clint bet another dollar. Kane called.

"He said a whole bunch of stuff I couldn't understand, but what it amounted to was I got a beauty of a scar on my thigh, and something inside that never did heal right. I can't really straighten the leg, although it will usually take all of my weight. Hey, I paired up. Bet two dollars."

Clint saw that Kane had a pair of sevens on the table, and he called the bet. It was then that he realized that he'd been so interested in Kane's story that he'd forgotten to look at his hold card. He did so now.

Kane dealt out the last card and bet five dollars.

"Raise five."

"I raise five also."

"I'll raise again."

"Okay, I'll call."

"Two pair," Kane said, revealing sevens and threes.

"Kings," Clint said. "Maybe your luck hasn't changed after all."

"My luck's been all bad ever since that bayonet went into my thigh," Kane said, taking his money and passing the deck to Clint. "What about you?"

"My luck?"

"Your story. How you got to be a living legend."

Clint made a face, but felt he owed the man something in return for his story. He explained how he'd come west from the East with an abiding interest in guns, how he'd studied them until he could take them apart, put them back together, and then interchange parts and make his own guns. He also explained how he got involved with the law, first as a deputy, then as a sheriff and a marshal, until finally he felt like giving it up and traveling.

"So you're actually a gunsmith now?" Kane asked. "A real, working gunsmith?"

"When I work."

"And you think that your ability with guns is just something you came by naturally?"

Clint shrugged. "I was pretty much always able to hit what I aimed at."

"But your speed. Surely you must practice."

"No. Anyone who has to practice better just forget about wearing a gun."

"The kid's pretty good, you know."

"Laramie?"

"Yeah."

"Does he practice?"

"All the time, but he's really pretty good."

"I saw him in the saloon the other night," Clint said.

"Not bad, huh?"

"He should have killed the man."

"He winged him. That was enough."

"You take time to make a fancy shot, and eventually somebody who's not as fancy is going to kill you."

"You're criticizing him for not killing a man?"

"If you draw your gun on a man, Gimpy, you better damn well kill him. You must have learned that by now."

"That's usually the case when I fire my gun," Kane said, nudging the Greener with his foot.

"Why a shotgun?"

"Unlike you," Kane said, "I could never hit what I aimed at. With this, I hardly ever miss."

"I can see why. Five-card stud again?"

"Deal."

Chapter Twenty-Four

Clint didn't get a chance to ask Kane how he came to be riding with Laramie Jones. Not then anyway. The next time they were left alone, however, he broached the subject.

"That's a story," Kane said, "and a right strange one."

"You willing to tell it?"

"Hell, why not?"

Kane even put the cards down to tell this one, although it wasn't very long.

"I was up in the Dakotas hunting wolf."

"Was this before or after your leg?"

"After, well after the war."

"And you were hunting wolf?"

"Man's got to make a living, Clint, and I reckon I've made mine in more ways than any man alive."

That's another story, Clint thought—a lot more stories.

"Anyway, I was hunting wolf and I found Laramie. He was naked and half dead."

"A wolf?"

"No, he'd obviously been beaten by a man, or by more than one man. There were no marks on him to indicate that he'd been attacked by a wolf."

"What happened?"

"I nursed him back to health."

"And did he tell you who did that to him?"

"He didn't know—in fact he didn't even know his name." Kane leaned forward and said, "And he still doesn't."

"But . . . he's Laramie Jones."

"We decided on that name, both of us. I always liked the town of Laramie, and he picked Jones. He said it would be easy to remember."

"How long ago was this?"

"Laramie Jones was born five years ago. He has no idea of what his life was like before that."

"Has he seen doctors?"

"He saw a lot of doctors in the beginning. Most of them didn't know what they were dealing with. We finally went to a specialist in Denver, and he said that Laramie had am—uh, aman . . ."

"Amnesia?"

"That's the one. He said that his memory could just come back one day, just like that, but that there was nothing we could do to make it come back."

"And you've been together ever since?"

"That we have. I'm the only family the boy knows. He was twenty-one when I found him, and almost everything he knows now I taught him."

"Except how to use a gun?"

"I taught him what I knew, and he went the rest of the way by himself. He said that nobody was ever going to give him a beating like that again. He's only afraid of two things in the world, that boy."

"What's that?"

"One is that he'll get amnesia again and forget the past five years."

"And the other?"

"The other . . . is that his memory will come back."

"Why would he be afraid of that?"

"He's afraid of what he might have been. I think at this point he's satisfied with the life he has as Laramie Jones. He'd rather not know who or what he was before."

"I guess I can understand that."

"Besides," Kane said, shuffling the cards again, "his name might be Orville or something. . . ."

"You staked a claim here?" Laramie Jones asked Joe Bags.

They were at Nina's, waiting for their food to be brought out, and Laramie was talking about Nina herself.

Bags was about to answer yes when he realized that he really did have no claim on Nina. If she found Laramie attractive and wanted to get involved with him, that was her business. Also, if she didn't find Laramie attractive and chose to stay with Bags, that was her business too.

And his.

"I don't know as I'd say I staked a claim, Laramie. Nina and I have gotten to be . . . close."

"I don't want to step on nobody's toes, Joe," Laramie said. "We didn't get on at first, but I guess I kind of like you."

Bags was surprised, because he'd begun to feel the same way as Laramie. Being cooped up for three days with each other might have that effect, Clint had said. Clint had also warned that if it stretched on for any longer than that, they might start to get on each other's nerves.

"I guess you'd just have to ask Nina herself, Laramie."

"Maybe I'll just forget it. I've made myself a pretty good friend over at Jenny Lee's."

"Oh yeah?"

"Her name's Marion—I think."

"Real good friends, huh?"

"Well, if you pay enough, she'd be your friend too," Laramie said, grinning.

"It's been three days," Simon Trehayne said to John Tobin.

"So?"

"How long are we going to wait?"

"Longer than I had first intended, since they're holed up in that jail—thanks to someone's aborted attempt on the sheriff's life."

His tone said that he knew Trehayne was behind the attempt, though he hadn't come out and said so during the past three days.

"Dallas has been in that jail for three days."

"Not that he doesn't deserve it."

Trehayne certainly agreed with that, although he chose not to say so.

"We'll wait a few days longer, Simon," John Tobin said. "Long enough for them to start getting on each other's nerves and start fighting amongst themselves. That's when we'll make our move."

"There could be a judge here by then."

"The nearest judge is two weeks away—if they were able to get him. If they had to get someone else, it will take even longer. We have plenty of time." Tobin's plan of waiting had been devised after that long night with Mary—or Marion, or whatever her name was. He'd been relaxed enough after that to think it over calmly and come to his present decision.

Wait.

Chapter Twenty-Five

After five days things weren't so friendly.

The poker game was over because Laramie Jones finally got fed up with losing and exploded. He and Clint almost came to blows simply because Clint chose to be the target for his anger. Kane was injured, and Bags was the sheriff. It wouldn't have done for Jones to have exchanged blows with an injured man or with the sheriff, and Clint didn't think anything would actually happen. He figured that being cooped up and losing at cards, Jones merely needed someone to vent his anger on.

After that, Kane and Bags started playing checkers while Clint worked on his guns—breaking them down, cleaning them—and then worked on everyone else's guns.

Jones, being the youngest of the four and accustomed to spending his nights in other ways, continued to become more and more irritable.

Finally, on the sixth night, Kane said, "Hey, Laramie."

"Yeah?"

"Why don't you do us all a favor? Go over to Jenny Lee's and work off some of your youthful impatience."

Jones looked at Kane, then at Bags and Clint.

"One of us could walk over there with him, make sure he doesn't get hurt," Clint said.

"You ain't seen the day a whore can hurt me."

"I wasn't talking about a whore."

"Why don't you come with me and get some yourself, Clint?"

"I'll come with you," Clint said, standing up, "but I'll wait for you downstairs."

"Gonna rush me, huh?"

"That's the only way you're going to do it."

Laramie looked at Kane, who nodded.

"Okay, let's go."

Clint walked over and gave Bags his gun, which he had been working on. "It won't pull to the left anymore. Remember that when you use it."

"I'll remember. Thanks."

"You have to jump," Clint said, pointing to the board.

Annoyed, Bags said, "I know that!"

Pretty soon, Clint thought, Bags was going to have to visit Nina and work off some of *his* youthful impatience.

"Let's go," he said to Laramie.

As they walked down the street, it was starting to get dark.

"Probably should have saved this for tomorrow, when it was lighter," Clint said, looking around.

"I won't be long," Laramie said. "That is, I'll try not to take long."

"If you do," Clint said, "I'll come up and get you."

It had been said in jest, but Jones gave him a quick look, and Clint saw something he didn't like. He thought that the time might come when Jones would want to try him, and hoped their period of waiting would come to an end before that happened.

Two days before, John Tobin had made another decision, this one also taking place after a relaxing session with Marion—or Mary or whatever. The decision was to have two men watch the sheriff's office from the roof of the building across the street and observe the movements of the men inside, keeping track of them. Tobin wanted to see if they were keeping any kind of schedule.

For two days the men noticed that two men left the office to pick up breakfast, lunch, and dinner, and that was all. Now they observed an unscheduled trip.

"What do we do?" one man asked.

"Follow them, see where they go," the other man said quickly. "If we get a chance, we take it."

"Those ain't our orders, Dick."

The other man gave the first man an annoyed look and said, "You ain't never gonna get anywhere in this world, Earl, if all you do is follow orders."

Clint waited downstairs with the rest of the girls while Laramie Jones went upstairs with a blond-haired girl named Marion—or Mary—he wasn't sure if he heard right.

Once or twice one of the other girls came over to him and made a pitch, and if either of them had been for free, he might have taken them up on it. Jenny Lee had some pretty decent-looking girls. Jenny Lee herself was in her mid-fifties. Voluptuous at one time in her life, she was now a blowsy, busty blonde with thickening waist and hips. Still and all, she probably would have given most men a roll for their money in bed. There was a lot to be said for experience.

After half an hour Jones came walking down the stairs alone. "How'd I do?" he asked.

"I was just about to come up and get you."

Again Clint noticed that look, as if Jones wanted to make an issue of the comment. Clint felt that Kane must have warned Jones to keep his temper in check. He'd probably even made a special point of telling him to temper himself around the Gunsmith.

He had to give the kid credit, Clint thought. He was making an effort. Any kid who thought he was good with a gun started to salivate around a man with a rep.

"Let's get back."

Jones nodded and they headed for the door.

Outside, they were about to step into the street when Clint heard a board creak.

"Down!" he shouted. If he was wrong, they'd look silly; if he was right, they'd be alive.

Jones obeyed, and the shots fired from each side missed.

"Take the right." Clint didn't have to speak loudly, because they were close together.

"Whose right?"

"Yours. Wait for the flash."

They rolled away from each other, each watching his own direction. There was a shot from Clint's side, and he saw the flash. He fired three quick shots and was rewarded with the sound of a man crying out.

From behind him he heard a shot, followed by two. He got up, ran in a crouch toward the flash, and had to stop short to keep from tripping over the body. He turned the man over and studied him in the moonlight. All three shots had hit him in the torso.

He turned and looked the other way, saw Jones running toward him.

"He got away, but I hit him. There's blood on the ground."

"Let's get back," Clint said, looking up and down the street, then up at the rooftops. "They might have been alone, but let's not count on it."

They moved quickly without running, and got back to the jail without further incident.

"What's wrong?" Bags asked as they entered.

Clint ejected the spent shells from his guns and fed in live ones, telling them what had happened.

"You know what that means," Kane said.

Bags frowned, but Clint said, "Yeah, Tobin had somebody watching us."

"Why just watch?"

"To see what kind of routine we keep."

"This wasn't part of any routine," Jones said. He reloaded also.

"I know. Somebody got ambitious. Laramie wounded one, and I don't know what he'll go home and tell Tobin, but we're going to have to be ready for anything."

"Why has he waited this long?" Laramie Jones asked.

"He wants us to get jumpy, start getting on each

other's nerves—and that's what we've been doing.
No more of that. I don't care what one of us does
that another doesn't like, we save that until this is all
over. Deal?''

"Deal," Bags said.

Kane nodded.

Clint looked at Jones, whose head was down as he
reloaded. When he looked up and saw the three of
them looking at him expectantly, he shrugged and
said, "Oh . . . deal."

"That's twice!" Tobin shouted.

"I had nothing to do with it, John," Simon
Trehayne said. "They went on their own."

"Where are they?"

"One died in the street, the other died here after he
told me what happened."

"All right. Get me some good men, Simon—some
good men, do you understand?"

"Yes."

"Have them here in three days. I'm not using any
more cowhands for this job."

"All right."

"Get as many as you think you'll need."

Trehayne nodded. He started to leave, but stopped
when a question occurred to him. "You want me to
have two men watch them again?"

"If you can get two men who can follow orders,
yes."

"I'll find two."

Trehayne left the house and walked to the livery,
where some of the men were setting down the body of
Dick Wilson. He stopped outside and let his hand fall
to his gun.

He'd get as many good men as he needed, and then he and they would do the job. First, though, he was going to have to renegotiate with his friend, John Tobin.

It was long past time for him to start looking after himself.

Chapter Twenty-Six

At the beginning of the second week of their self-imposed incarceration, the four men were actually getting along even better than they had during the first days. They did not, however, start the poker game again.

In the back room, in the cells, Dallas Tobin had taken to carrying on. He'd shout and yell until he was hoarse, then stop until he regained his voice, and start again. Half the time he was cursing them out for putting him in that cell for over a week, and the other half of the time he was cursing his father for leaving him there.

"You know, I'm starting to wonder," Bags said.

"About what?" Clint asked.

"I'm starting to wonder if we haven't built this thing up more than it's worth."

Bags and Clint were in the office alone, as Jones had taken Gimpy Kane out for some exercise, and to pick up lunch for everyone.

"You'd better explain that."

"Well, maybe the old man just ain't coming, Clint. Maybe he intends to leave his son right here and let him pay for what he did."

Clint thought a moment, then shook his head. "I can't believe that."

"Why not?"

"Because we're dealing with blood here."

"You're saying that if it was your son in that cell, you'd bust him out?"

"I might."

"I can't believe that. Why hasn't he tried anything yet?"

"There *were* two incidents."

"Both of which could have been men trying to get on John Tobin's good side. I mean, he didn't necessarily have to have anything to do with those attempts."

"That's true, but I still think he'll come."

"Maybe he'll wait too long," Bags said, "and the judge will get here first."

"I don't think it matters," Clint said. "Tobin won't let his son go to trial."

"You seem pretty sure."

"I've dealt with men like him before," Clint said, "and if you're going to continue being a sheriff— here or anywhere else—you're going to deal with a lot of men like John Tobin."

"Well, then, this'll be a learning experience."

At that point a voice called out from outside. "Hello the jail!"

It was Laramie Jones.

Clint moved to the door to unlock it and admit Jones and Kane. "About time," he said, "I'm starved."

"Ain't we all," Kane said.

"How's the shoulder?" Clint asked.

"Stiff, like the leg."

Kane limped over to a chair and settled himself into it.

Laramie Jones went over to Bags's desk and put down the two paper bags he was carrying. "Sandwiches," he said.

"What kind?" Bags asked.

"Chicken."

"Bring them theirs," Bags said, indicating the back room, where the prisoners were in their cells.

"You know," Jones said, taking out two sandwiches for the prisoners, "I kind of feel sorry for the big guy."

"Why?"

"He was just doing what the other one, Tobin, told him to do. I get the feeling he always does what somebody tells him to do."

"Yeah, well, give him his sandwich and tell him to eat it," Kane said irritably. Clint felt that Kane wasn't annoyed at one of them so much as he was at his injuries. He had a feeling that not only was the shoulder bothering him, but the leg as well. "And if that other one starts yelling again, tell him I'm gonna come back there, stuff both barrels up his ass, and pull the triggers."

Jones made a face at Bags and took the two sandwiches back to Dallas Tobin and Luke Joyner.

Clint took a sandwich, walked over to where Kane was sitting and asked, "How you doing?"

"I ache."

"The shoulder?"

Kane looked up at Clint and said, "More like the leg. Something's gonna happen, I can feel it."

"What are we talking about here? The weather?"

"I wish I was. I don't know, my leg just acts sometimes when something bad is coming."

"I find that very comforting."

Clint left Kane there, massaging his leg, and went back to Bags's desk for his sandwich.

"What's the matter with him?"

"His leg hurts."

"Maybe he's getting impatient, like me. How do you stay so calm?"

"If something's going to happen, it'll happen. Eat your sandwich."

Three days later Simon Trehayne walked into John Tobin's office without knocking first.

"Simon?"

"We have to talk."

"About what?"

"A new deal."

"What do you mean? Did you get the men you need, as I asked?"

"I did."

"Are you ready to move then?"

"Not yet."

"Why not?"

"Like I said, we have to talk about a new deal."

"I don't understand. If there's something you want, why don't you just say it?"

"I want to stop playing nursemaid to that spoiled brat of yours."

"Simon . . ." Tobin said warningly.

"You know he's spoiled, John."

"He's still my son, and you're my employee—"

"Yes, I am, and I want to renegotiate my salary."

"Your salary? Oh, I see." Tobin thought he did see. Trehayne wanted some extra for getting his son out of jail. "How much do you want then?"

"A hundred thousand dollars."

"What?" Tobin asked in disbelief.

"That's my asking price for breaking your worthless son out of jail. Is he worth it to you?"

"I don't understand."

"I'll explain. The men I've gotten for you will cost ten thousand dollars each."

"And the other fifty?"

"That's mine. That's my reward for putting up with Dallas all these years."

"And then what? I mean, after you break him out and I pay you. You don't expect to come back here and work for me, do you?"

"No," Trehayne said, "I don't."

Tobin looked surprised.

"Is it a deal?"

For a few moments Tobin studied the man he thought he knew very well. "Why, Simon? After all these years."

"It's time, John," Trehayne said, moving toward the door. "It's just time. Let me know what you decide later today. If it's yes, be ready to let me know when you can have the money."

"The money!"

"We'll want all of the money before we go in, John," Trehayne said, "or you can try and go in yourself with your cowhands."

When Trehayne exited the house there were five impatient men waiting out front with their horses. They had come a lot of miles from different directions to see if they would be working together for ten thousand dollars a man.

Standing in front of the barn were six or seven of John Tobin's men, all of whom were impressed in one way or another by the strangers.

"Who are they?" one asked.

"I don't know all of them," another said, "but the tall one with the black leather gloves and string tie is Gentleman Harry Walker."

"Walker? I thought he was dead."

"Well, he ain't if he's standin' right over there, is he?"

"I know that man!" a third one said.

"Which one?"

"The heavyset one, the one who looks like a boxer."

The man he was talking about was about five-eight, with huge, sloping shoulders and large hands.

"He don't even look like he can handle a gun with them big hands."

"Are you kidding? That's Big Sam Piper."

"Piper?"

. . . and Del Apollo, a small man with fast hands and a quick temper . . .

. . . and Chico Santana, a handsome Mexican with a mean streak . . .

. . . and Dog Kelly, a man who preferred knives to guns, and wore six of them on his belt, all balanced for throwing. . . .

All gunmen with reputations, all for hire for an asking price of ten thousand dollars.

And they had been asked. . . .

Trehayne came down the steps and faced the five, impatient men.

"Did he go for it?" Walker asked. He'd apparently been elected spokesman for the group.

"We'll find out later today," Trehayne said. "Come on, I'll show you where to bed down your horses."

Walker grabbed the foreman's arm and said, "I'm coming out of retirement for this one, you know, Trehayne."

Trehayne looked at him and said, "After this one we'll all be able to retire."

Chapter Twenty-Seven

"Can I talk to you for a minute?" Dallas Tobin asked as Laramie Jones handed his lunch through the bars.

"Talk."

Tobin looked over at Joyner, who was asleep in the other cell.

"It can be worth a lot of money to you to get me out of here," Dallas Tobin said. "A lot of money."

"Oh, yeah? How much is a lot?"

"Name it."

"Fifty thousand dollars."

"Why not a hundred?"

"All right, a hundred."

"I was kidding."

"I'm not."

"Look," Tobin said, trying again, "let's talk seriously. I can pay you, say, ten thousand dollars to get me out of here before the judge gets here."

"Which should be any day now, shouldn't it? I mean, you have been here a long time now, haven't you?"

"All right, twenty-five thousand. That's as high as I can go."

"Are we talking about how high you can go, or how high your old man can go?"

Tobin snorted. "If I could depend on my old man, would I still be here?"

"I don't know, you tell me."

"Forget it. I'm talking about my money."

"Which you get from your father."

Tobin shook his head, then looked past Jones to see if they were in danger of being interrupted. He also looked at Joyner again, to make sure he was asleep.

Lowering his voice, he said, "It's my money. It was left to me by my mother."

"Where is it?"

"In the bank."

"I see. I break you out of here, and then we walk over to the bank and make a withdrawal, hmm?"

"I'll get you the money!"

Jones looked over at the sleeping man and asked, "What about him?"

"He's asleep. He doesn't have to know anything about this."

"He's your partner, isn't he?"

"My partner?" Tobin had thought of Joyner as many things, but never his partner.

"Yeah, your partner. Sorry, Tobin, forget it."

"What do you mean, forget it?"

"A man doesn't sell out his partner," Jones said, moving toward the door. "When he wakes up tell him to call me, and I'll bring him his lunch."

"Hey," Tobin said in a hoarse whisper, "hey!"

Clint and Bags were playing checkers at Bags's

desk while Kane sat rubbing a cloth over the barrel of his shotgun.

"Has Dallas offered you money yet to let him go?" Clint asked Bags.

"No, why?"

"Just wondering."

Bags looked over his shoulder and said, "Laramie's been in there a long time giving them lunch."

"Yup."

"You think Dallas is offering him money?"

"It's a possibility."

"You think he'll take it?"

"It's a possibility."

"You're a big help."

"Where are the cell keys?"

"In my drawer."

"Are they there?"

Bags rolled his chair back, opened the desk, peered in, closed it, rolled his chair back and said, "Yes."

"Then it's your jump."

"What took you so long?" Kane asked as Jones came back into the office.

"Tobin was offering me money to let him out."

"How much?"

"A lot."

"How much."

Looking embarrassed, Jones said, "Uh, twenty-five thousand dollars."

"And you said no?"

"I didn't say I said no."

"What did you say?"

"No."

"Why not?"

"I think," Jones said, as if he wasn't really sure, "if he had offered me the money to let both of them out, I might have taken it."

"Why didn't you?"

"The big kid's his partner, Gimp," Jones said, "and he was going to let him rot in jail. You don't turn on your partner that way."

"Who taught you that?"

"You did."

Looking doubtful, Gimpy Kane shook his head and said, "I never taught you to turn down no twenty-five thousand dollars."

"Gimp, what would I do with twenty-five thousand dollars?"

"Lose it at poker."

Jones nodded and said, "Exactly."

That night John Tobin sent for his former foreman and friend, Simon Trehayne.

"All right, Simon, I agree to your terms."

"And the money?"

"Yes, but I want you to know one thing though."

"What's that?"

"Once you've been paid, I don't want to see you on this property."

"That won't be a problem, John," Simon said.

"I don't have that much here. I'll have to go to the bank tomorrow and get it."

"That's fine. We'll just ride into town and back with you. That's a lot of money for you to be carrying around all by yourself."

"That won't be necessary."

"Sure it will. My men will want to get a look at the jail, and at the men they'll be . . . going up against."

Tobin narrowed his eyes and asked, "Have you told them they'll have to be going up against the Gunsmith?"

"No."

"Why not?" Tobin demanded with a knowing look. "Were you afraid they wouldn't agree to try and break Dallas out?"

"No," Trehayne said. "I was afraid that if I told them, they'd offer to do it for free."

Chapter Twenty-Eight

The next morning seven men rode down the main street of Rio Malo. Two rode ahead of the others, while the remaining five were bunched up behind them.

Clint Adams and Joe Bags were making the breakfast run when they spotted the riders. They were about to go into the café when Clint grabbed Bags's arm. They paused in front of the café, Clint knowing that the riders would have to pass them and that he could get a good look at them. He wanted to be sure he was seeing right.

"What is it?" Bags asked.

"Watch."

"That's Tobin and his foreman, isn't it?"

"It sure is."

"And who are those men behind them? They don't look like cowhands."

"They're not," Clint said. "They're gunhands."

"You know them?"

"Some of them—and they know me. Back into the doorway a bit. I don't want them to see me just yet."

"Tobin must have told them by now who they're going up against."

"Maybe not. Let's watch."

As they rode by, Clint identified the men he knew. "The Mexican, that's Chico Santana."

"I haven't heard of him."

"If you had spent any time in Mexico you would have. The thickest fella there, that's Big Sam Piper. You've heard of him, haven't you?"

"Now him I've heard of. It looks like Tobin's gone out and hired himself some big guns."

"You haven't heard the biggest," Clint said. "The tall man with the gloves and the tie?"

"Yeah?"

"That's Harry Walker."

"Gentleman Harry Walker?"

"The same."

"Does he know you?"

"He and Piper do, yeah."

"Have you faced them?"

Clint shook his head. "I've seen them in action though. Walker's the faster of the two, but Piper has the added asset of his strength. He's an extremely powerful man, and he doesn't need a gun to kill you."

"What about the other two?"

"I don't know them by sight, but I'm sure I'll recognize their names when I hear them."

"And they'll know you?"

"Probably."

"If they don't know what they're going up against, what will happen when they're told? Will they change their minds and not take the job?"

"I'll tell you one of the curses of having a reputation, Joe. With that bunch, they're each going to want to have a try at me."

"Will you face them each?"

"If I had to, I would . . . until one of them killed me."

"Or until you killed all of them."

"And that's the curse, right there."

"Clint, with what we've got, how would we hold them all off if they came at one time?"

"We've got an edge, Joe."

"What edge?"

"We're on the inside and they're on the outside. That jail is like a fort."

"You know how many forts have been slaughtered?"

"Let's not talk about that now. We've got to get breakfast and get back to tell the others."

"Where do you suppose they're going?" Joe asked, lagging behind as Clint started through the café door. Clint stopped and stepped out again.

"Knowing the money it would take to hire that much talent, I'd say they were headed for the bank."

Clint was about to go into the café when Harry Walker's eyes slid over his way and fastened on his. There was no doubt about it. Walker had seen him.

And recognized him.

"Let's go," he said, and entered the café.

Walker urged his horse on until he was riding abreast of Trehayne. Trehayne, smart enough to know something was wrong, lagged behind, allowing John Tobin to forge ahead.

"What are you trying to pull?"

"What do you mean?"

"I mean the Gunsmith."

Trehayne looked around, either looking for the

Gunsmith or looking to see if the others could hear him. "You saw him?"

"I saw him . . . and he saw me. When were you going to tell us, Trehayne?"

"After we got paid."

"Afraid we'd ask for more?"

"You wouldn't have done that."

"No, we wouldn't have," Walker said. "At least, I wouldn't have—but I am now."

"Why?"

"Because I don't like being hired in the dark. I want to know what I'm going up against right up front."

"And now that you do?"

"I want a bigger piece of the pie, Trehayne, or the deal's off."

"You can't do that."

"I can't? Watch me. All I've got to do is talk to the others and they'll go along with me."

They rode in silence for a few moments, and as they approached the bank Trehayne finally spoke.

"Oh, all right. I'll pay you twenty thousand—but you've got to keep the others from wanting more."

"Don't worry about a thing, Trehayne," Walker said. "You play fair with me and I'll play fair with you. We trust each other, right?"

Usually Clint and Bags waited at a table while Nina went to the kitchen for their breakfast, lunch, or dinner.

This time, however, when they entered the café, Nina said, "Joe, could you come into the kitchen and help me?"

"Uh, sure, Nina."

"Go ahead," Clint said, his mind still on the procession of gunmen that had just ridden by.

Bags followed Nina into the kitchen and said, "What do you need help with?"

"Nothing. The food is all prepared."

"Then what did you—"

She turned into him and kissed him hard, thrusting her tongue into his mouth.

"Nina, wha—"

"I want you, Joe. This is going on too long. Just when we found each other, you had to go into hiding in the jail. It isn't fair."

"Nina, I want you, too, but I can't—I don't have the time—"

"You have time for this," she said, her hand on the bulge inside his pants.

"Nina . . ."

Anxiously she began to unbutton his pants. That done, she reached inside, groped for him, and pulled out his rigid penis.

"Nina . . ."

"I can't get the rest of you out," she said, "but this will do."

She caught him in her mouth and began to suck on him, kneading his balls through his pants.

"Nina . . . Jesus . . ."

He wondered if Clint could hear anything outside. To him, Nina sounded as if she were moaning so *loud*, and soon he was trying to contain his own moans of pleasure.

Nina continued to work on him, using her lips and her teeth, licking the underside of his prick slowly and lovingly, then swallowing it up again and sucking it until he thought he'd cry out loud.

And then he came and felt as if his head had exploded. She continued to suck him even then, drawing more from him when he could have sworn there was no more, and then she released him, sat back on her heels and smiled at him, licking her lips.

"Was that so bad?"

"Jesus," he said, tucking himself away and closing his pants.

She stood up and said, "I'll get your food," as if nothing had happened.

When Bags came out with the food his legs were shaking, and he wondered if Clint could tell.

Chapter Twenty-Nine

Jones and Kane reacted well to the news that Tobin had hired professional gunmen.

"Well, at least we know our waiting is almost at an end," Jones said. "With those guns in town it won't be long before they make a move."

"What's on your mind?" Joe Bags asked Gimpy Kane. The older man was looking pensively at the floor.

"I know Sam Piper."

"How well?" Clint asked.

Kane looked up and said, "If he finds out I'm in here, he'll tear down the door with his bare hands."

"Why?" Bags asked.

"Ten years ago I killed his brother."

"How did that happen?" Jones asked.

"I blew him in half . . . with this," Kane said, indicating the shotgun.

"I think Laramie meant to ask what caused it."

Kane shrugged. "Piper's brother was trying to rape a girl in an alley. I called him on it and he turned and went for his gun. He didn't leave me any choice."

"Was Sam in town?"

"No, my understanding is that he came into town later and found out."

"Who was the girl?" Jones asked.

"Just some prostitute."

"Piper wouldn't forget something like that."

"I know."

"You've been running from him ever since?" Laramie Jones asked. The look on his face was one of disappointment in the man who had been his friend, father, and mentor for the past five years.

"Let me answer that, Gimpy," Clint said. He faced Jones and said, "You'd better smarten up some, son. It would have taken a fool to wait in that town for Sam Piper to show up. My guess is that it was just time to leave, and Gimpy left. If Piper's been on the lookout for him these past ten years, that's no surprise, but I'm sure he hasn't been searching all this time, and I'm damn sure Gimpy Kane hasn't been running."

Jones looked embarrassed then, and turned to Kane.

"Gimp, I'm sorry—"

"Forget it, kid. Let's decide how we're going to play this."

"Clint thinks they'll each want to call him out," Bags said, "and we can't let that happen. That's putting too much pressure on Clint. If they call for a face off, it's got to be all of us." He looked at Kane and asked, "You up to that?"

"Yes."

"We can't do it that way," Clint said.

"Why not?"

"That would leave the office empty."

"Then one of us would have to stay here while the

others go out into the street," Bags said.

"How do we decide who goes and who stays?" Jones asked. "Draw straws?"

"That won't work either."

Bags showed a flash of annoyance on his face. "Why not?"

"Because that would leave *one* person here, which isn't enough to . . . hold the fort."

"Then what do you suggest?"

"Well, if they want me, I'll face them one at a time."

"You can't do that."

"Why not?"

"Because I'm the sheriff. Besides, you're not even a deputy."

"So deputize him" Jones said.

Bags looked at Jones and said, "We've been all through that."

"Then what?" Jones asked.

Bags looked around and said, "One of us will have to back Clint up."

"We're back to the beginning," Jones said. "How do we decide. Draw straws?"

"I'll take Kane," Clint said.

"Why?" Jones asked.

"Don't get insulted," Clint said. "The prisoners are Bags's responsibility. If anything happens to them, it's his badge. If anything happens to me, it's my business, because I'm just a private citizen."

"And what's wrong with me?"

"No experience."

"Kane's busted up—" Bags began.

"Kane's an old warhorse. Busted up, he's even more dangerous."

164

"I don't like it."

"Also, when Piper sees Kane, all hell may break loose. That'll give me an edge."

Bags couldn't argue that. Jones wanted to, but he couldn't either.

Clint looked at Kane. "You game?"

"Sure."

"You fit?"

"Hell, yes."

"Sorry to hear it."

The five hired gunmen waited outside the bank while John Tobin and Simon Trehayne went inside. Trehayne stood alongside Tobin while he withdrew the money.

"I'm supposed to notify the manager when there is a withdrawal of this size, Mr. Tobin," the young woman teller said, somewhat timidly.

"Just give me my money, young lady. I own a good percentage of this bank."

"But my job—"

"I'll have your job if you don't give me my money."

"Are you . . . all right. Sir?" she asked, eyeing Trehayne.

"This man is my foreman, damn it! Now give me my goddamn money!"

"Y-yes, sir."

When Tobin had his money, he and Trehayne turned and started for the door.

"We'll go back to the ranch and I'll pay you and the others what—"

"No," Trehayne said. "Outside."

"In front of the whole town?" Tobin asked, aghast. "But why?"

"Because we're here already. There's no point in going back to your ranch. Also, because they can see us from the jailhouse."

"You want them to see me paying you and those ... gunmen?"

"That's right."

"If I didn't know you better, Trehayne," Tobin said, staring at Trehayne with a puzzled look, "I'd say you were using psychology."

"Who says you ever knew me?"

"Look at this," Jones said. He was standing at the window of the office that looked out on to the main street.

Clint and Bags walked over to the window. Kane didn't bother, because they all wouldn't have fit. Besides, his leg was hurting.

"What is it?" Bags asked.

"Tobin. He's handing out a bunch of money right on the street in front of the bank."

From the window they could see John Tobin not indiscriminately doling out a considerable amount of cash to the five gunmen ... and his foreman!

"He's paying his foreman too?" Bags asked. "The man works for him. I can see him paying the others, but why his foreman?"

"Maybe he's gone into business for himself," Clint said. "It wouldn't be the first time."

"What do you know about Trehayne?" Jones asked.

"Just the name, some years back. He wasn't

always a ranch foreman."

"He was a hired gun?"

"For a short time."

"What happened?"

"He changed professions. And now I guess he's changed back."

Chapter Thirty

Bags and Jones made the dinner run while Clint and Kane waited in the office.

"Should we tell the kid?" Kane said.

"Tell him what?" Clint asked.

"That his father has hired six big, bad gunmen to bust him out."

"Let him find out for himself."

Kane shrugged his indifference. The door opened and Bags and Jones entered with hot dinner on two trays.

"I'll give them theirs," Clint said, taking one of the trays. There were three stew dinners on it, one for each of the prisoners and the remaining one for him.

"I'll make coffee," Bags said.

"Fine."

Clint went in the back, ignored the remarks of Dallas Tobin and the baleful look of Luke Joyner as he gave them their meals, and then returned to the office to eat his.

"They're in the saloon," Bags said.

"Which one?" Clint asked.

"April's."

"Uh-huh," Clint replied, sitting down with the tray in his lap and attacking his stew. "I'll get to them right after I eat."

"What for?"

"They're over there waiting for me," Clint said. "I can't disappoint them."

"You're going with him," Bags said to Kane.

The older man shook his head.

"This time he goes alone. Next time I'll go along with him."

"What's he talking about?"

"They're just going to want to talk to me," Clint said, "feel me out. See if it's really me."

"And what do you want to do? Walk in there like some strutting, fighting cock? Why don't we go over there and take them, front and back."

"That ain't the way it's done," Kane said. "I don't back shoot nobody."

"I'll be fine," Clint said, setting his tray aside and standing up. "We're just going to have a talk, Walker and me."

"Walker? Why him?"

"He'll be the spokesman for the others."

"Why him?"

"Because he hasn't just got a gun, he's got a brain too. He'll think and talk for the others. Also, this way I'll be able to find out who the others are. We'll know who we're dealing with."

Bags looked at Kane, who said, "It makes sense."

Jones nodded his agreement.

"Go, damn it."

"This is me," Clint said, moving toward the door, "going."

· · ·

When Clint Adams walked into the room, all six men saw him immediately.

Simon Trehayne was seated at a table in the back. He was out of this part, just a spectator.

Harry Walker was at a table by the bar, looking as dapper as ever.

The other four were standing at the bar, Sam Piper taking up as much room as any two of them.

Clint walked over to Walker's table.

"Hello, Clint."

"Harry."

"Have a seat."

The Gunsmith sat down.

"Sam, bring my friend a drink."

"A beer," Clint said.

He looked around, surprised that the bartender was nowhere to be found and that the place was empty at this time of the evening. Then he remembered that John Tobin owned a piece of the place.

Where was April? he wondered.

Sam Piper brought the beer and put it down in front of Clint.

"Hello, Sam."

Piper didn't reply, and went back to his place at the bar.

"Sam's his old talkative self, huh?"

"When he has something to say. Actually, he's real glad to see you."

"I'll bet he is."

Walker was Clint's age and his approximate build, but he dressed better than Clint ever had. He always wore white shirts, black string ties, and a flat-

brimmed black hat. His hands were always clean—
something that was difficult when you were a working gunsmith. It might also have had something to do
with the fact that he almost always wore those leather
gloves, Clint thought. Walker didn't have them on
now, and his hands were clean.

He looked more like a gambler than a gunman.

"You must be getting paid a bundle for this,
Harry. I heard you retired."

"I tried. I thought I had enough money to make it
stick, but I've got expensive tastes."

"I can understand that."

"I didn't know you were in on this when I came."

"I kind of figured that."

Gentleman Harry regarded the Gunsmith silently
for a few moments, punctuating the moment with a
sip of his whiskey.

"Clint . . . can you walk away from this one?"

Now Clint regarded Gentleman Harry over his
glass for not quite as long and said, "Not likely,
Harry."

Walker stroked his upper lip with his thumb and
gave an exasperated sigh.

"Afraid I can't either, Clint. Like you said, I'm
getting paid a lot of money for this one. What about
you?"

"The sheriff's a friend of mine."

"Well . . . if you've got to die, it might as well be
for a friend, right?"

"I suppose that's as good a reason as any."

They both paused to sip their drinks.

"I know Sam, Harry," Clint said, "and Chico
Santana, there, but who are these other boys?"

"The little one, he's Del Apollo. He's real sensitive about his size . . . or lack of it. If Sam Piper said anything to him about it, he'd go after Sam. Imagine that? He's got himself a mean temper."

"Guess he isn't any smarter than he is tall, huh?"

Clint felt the little man stiffen, but a look from Walker kept him still.

"The one with all the blades, well, that's Dog Kelly. His parents named him Dog because when he was born they could tell he was mean as a dog."

Kelly was a thin, almost emaciated man of indeterminate age. He might even have had some Indian blood. From the slack appearance of his mouth, Clint guessed that he had little or no teeth.

"Jesus, he's ugly."

"He knows that."

Walker looked at the four men standing at the bar and said, for the sake of Apollo and Kelly, "Gentlemen, this is Clint Adams, the Gunsmith."

"Charmed," Clint said.

"How many men you got in there with you, Clint?"

"They must have told you that, Harry."

"They said two deputies and the sheriff."

"I'd hardly call them deputies," Clint said. "I've got a cripple and an inexperienced kid."

Walker smiled and said, "You're deriding your own men, Clint. Why does that make me wary?"

"Would I lie to you, Harry?"

"I think we've done all the talking we need to do. How do you want to play this?"

"You might rush the jail."

Walker shook his head. "Not my style, Clint. If I

rushed it you could hole up in there for days."

"We already have."

"Getting tired of it?"

"Yes."

"I checked on the judge."

That surprised Clint. "And?"

"There's only one serving this area, and he's over-worked. He still won't be here for a week. Can you last another week cooped up in there?"

"We may have to."

"No, you don't."

"What do you suggest?"

"The street."

"Me against the five"—Clint began, then looked past Walker at Trehayne and said—"the six of you?"

"No, you've got four guns, we'll send four guns out, and it'll be a fair fight. How about it? We'll get this thing wrapped up real quick. Maybe we could even go one against one with you until one of us beats you."

"When would you go, Harry?" Clint asked. "First . . . or last."

"Me? I've seen your move, Clint. Given the choice I'd go last . . . but we'd probably draw straws."

"You've already been paid, Harry," Clint said. "You could ride out now."

Again Walker shook his head and said, "Not my style, Clint. I hired on to do a job, and I've got to do it. This is going to be the last."

Clint stood up and said, "It could be the last for a lot of us, Harry. I'll let you know what we decide."

"The time for discussing things is over, Clint.

We'll be on the street at sunup tomorrow. We'll expect you to be there as well."

"Thanks for the beer."

"My pleasure."

Clint looked at Trehayne, who boldly returned his gaze, and then left the saloon.

He still wondered where April was.

Chapter Thirty-One

After Clint Adams left the Dancer House Saloon, Gentleman Harry Walker stood up, walked over to Simon Trehayne's table, and sat down.

"You gave him a chance to walk away?"

"We explored the possibility."

"And he turned it down?"

"I expected him to."

"Then why did you give him the offer?"

"Because I had to."

"I don't understand that."

"I don't expect you to. You weren't in the business long enough to know the rules, Trehayne."

"Rules?" Trehayne said, laughing. "There are rules to being a gunman?"

"Oh, they're not written down in a book or anything like that, but they're there. Sometimes we bend 'em a little, but most of the time we play by them."

"Sounds like something that could get you killed."

"Oh, that happens too," Walker said. "A lot. You didn't hang around long enough to see much of that either."

"I decided that it wasn't for me."

"And you decided early. That's real good." Walker leaned forward and asked, "And what decided you to come back to it now?"

"I'm not. It's just going to be this once, and then I'll have enough money to do what I want."

"Just this once," Walker repeated, and Trehayne nodded. "I heard you were pretty good."

"I was."

"Lose it?"

"That's something you don't lose."

"I phrased it wrong. I know you don't lose it, but it can get rusty from lack of use."

"It's not rusty."

"Oh, no? Lots of practice behind the old barn, huh? Plinking empty bottles off the fence? Bottles don't shoot back, friend—"

"I hired you to back me up, Walker, not lecture me."

"Well, you've got to depend on me," Walker said, "and I've got to depend on you. I want to be sure you're gonna be there when the lead starts to fly."

"Hey, I'll be there, Walker," Trehayne said. "Just make sure you and your friends are there."

"They're not my friends," Walker said, "and we'll be there."

"I can't lose sight of the fact that you've already been paid."

"None of us is gonna walk with the money, Trehayne."

"That's what you told me."

"I'm not used to having my word questioned."

"Fine. Be there, and I won't question you."

"Oh, I'll be there, I wouldn't miss this for the world." Walker stood up to leave. "As good as you used to be, though, you'd better be a lot better now. A lot better.''

Clint went up the steps to April's door and knocked, hoping she'd open it. That would mean she was safe.

She did, and she was.

"Clint. Are those men—"

"They're still downstairs."

"Oooh, I'm furious!" she raged. She turned from the door and stalked into her apartment. Clint followed and shut the door.

"They pushed me out of my own place."

"Trehayne?"

"Trehayne said that John Tobin wanted me to turn the place over to those men for as long as they wanted. He even said they'd keep it open. Nobody's going to drink in a saloon that's filled with gunmen. They'd be afraid of being hit by a stray bullet. They could put me out of business!"

"One night won't put you out of business."

"Who says they'll only be there one night? They could be there for—"

"One night. By tomorrow they'll be gone."

"But they—wait a minute," she said, her eyes narrowing shrewdly. "They're here for you, aren't they?"

"They're here to break Dallas Tobin out of jail, if they can."

"And you're going to try and stop them."

"Yes."

"Let them have him, Clint," she said, rushing to him and grabbing him by the arms. "He isn't worth dying for."

"Who said I was going to die?"

"You can't stand against that many guns."

"I won't be alone."

"It doesn't matter. They'll kill you."

He removed her hands from his arms and said, "Tomorrow your place will be yours again."

"I'd let them keep it if it would keep you alive."

"By this time tomorrow your place and my life will still be around. I promise."

It was a promise he sincerely hoped he could keep.

Trehayne waited patiently and eventually was rewarded when Gentleman Harry Walker stood up and left the saloon, apparently to turn in for the night.

The other four seemed content to stand at the bar and drink, but Trehayne had something else in mind for them.

"Boys," he said, coming up behind them, "let me talk to you about something. . . ."

"So, what happened?" Jones asked when Clint came back to the office.

"They gave me a chance to walk away."

"Who did? Trehayne?" Bags asked.

"Walker. Trehayne didn't talk, he just watched."

"Did he offer you money?" Jones asked.

"He was offering me my *life*," Clint said.

"And you turned him down," Kane said. "I always said you were a good guy, Clint. Not too smart, but good."

"Thanks, Kane. Coming from the guy who's going out into the street with me tomorrow, that means a lot."

"Fuck a donkey, Adams."

"I'll have a cup of your coffee, Gimpy," Clint said. "It has about the same appeal."

Bags joined Clint at the stove and said, "I have an idea."

"An idea for what?"

"A way that you and Gimpy won't have to go out on the street alone tomorrow."

Clint turned, handed Bags a cup of coffee and said, "An idea like that I'm interested in hearing."

Chapter Thirty-Two

The next morning as the sun came up, Clint Adams and Gimpy Kane stepped out of the sheriff's office and found six men waiting in the street for them.

Trehayne, Walker, and the others were stretched across the street, Trehayne and Walker on either side, the other four in between, actually standing in the street.

"Three guns in the street," Clint said. "Dog Kelly likes knives."

"Which one's Kelly."

"The ugly one."

"That's a *real* big help."

"I'll see you in a little while," Clint said, stepping into the street.

"Yeah, send me a telegram when you get there."

Clint walked out into the center of the street, and Walker perked up.

"All alone, Clint?"

"I've got a proposition for you, Harry."

"What is it?"

"Me against one of your men, winner take all."

"An interesting proposition," Walker replied, "considering how outgunned you are."

"You may have the advantage in guns," Clint said, "but we've got the advantage as far as position."

"What position?" Walker asked, laughing. "You're in the middle of the street. You might as well be out in the middle of nowhere."

"Not quite right, Harry."

"What are you talking—"

Before Walker could finish there was a barrage of shots from the roof on either side of the street and the dirt at the feet of the four hired guns was chewed up by lead.

The four men were frozen, concerned that if they went for their guns, the lead would come their way instead of landing at their feet. They were smart enough to know that they were not being shot *at* —not yet anyway.

"What the—" Walker said. From his vantage point he looked up and saw a man with a badge on the roof of the jailhouse. Trehayne, on the other hand, could see Sheriff Joe Bags on the roof of the feed store on Walker's side of the street.

That meant that Dallas Tobin was unguarded!

"Don't move, Trehayne," Clint said as the foreman started to walk away. "I know what you've got in mind, but your business is out here in the street. Besides, don't worry about Dallas. He's being well taken care of."

"What are you up to, Adams?" Trehayne asked.

"Like I said before, we're outgunned, but we've got the best position. I'm offering you a chance to put one of your men up against me—or even you yourself. Who am I talking to here, who's in charge? You Harry, or Trehayne?"

"I'm in charge, Clint," Harry Walker said.

"No, I am!" Trehayne said, stepping into the street.

"I've been paid, Trehayne," Walker said. "I'm in charge here—"

"I don't need you anymore, Walker," Trehayne said. "If it's going to be one man against one man, then I can handle this alone."

Walker and Trehayne were glaring at each other now, the Gunsmith forgotten for the moment.

"Trehayne, don't be a fool—"

"I'll go through you, Walker—"

"You're making a mistake!" Walker shouted. "You're upset because Adams has outflanked you. Let me do what you're paying me to do."

"Stand back, Walker!"

Walker looked at Clint and said, "I told him didn't I?"

"You told him."

Good act, too, Clint thought.

"Let's go, Trehayne."

"Get off the street!" Trehayne told the other five.

"Let's leave them where they are, Trehayne. You wouldn't want me to give up my advantage, would you?"

"I thought you wanted to go man to man?"

"The question is, do you?"

"If you miss, you might hit one of them," Trehayne said lamely.

"Don't worry, Trehayne," Clint said, "I won't miss—and you can't be too confident in yourself if that's the way you're thinking."

"Never mind my confidence."

"Get out into the middle of the street then."

Trehayne took a few steps toward the center of the street, threw a glance at each of the men on the roof, and stopped.

"Oh, don't worry about them, Trehayne. They're just there to keep an eye on your men. This will just be between you and me. I guarantee it."

Trehayne's temper, which had gotten the better of him when he realized he'd been outsmarted, had waned, and now he was having second thoughts. Clint could see that.

So could Gentleman Harry Walker.

"Trehayne, why don't you get back up on the walk and let me do my job?"

Trehayne was torn between salvaging his pride or his life.

Walker stepped off the walk and strode to the center of the street. "All right, Clint. Come on, let's get this over with. I want to start spending my money."

"Why not let him do it himself, Harry?"

"He's the man who paid me, Clint," Walker said, "and I happen to know that you would gun him before he could clear leather. If I let that happen to an employer, I'd have a bad rep."

"I thought you were retiring after this?"

"That's beside the point. Come on, let's do this."

Clint faced Walker square, leaving it to Kane, Jones, and Bags to watch the other men. Kane had moved farther down the walk so that his shotgun would have maximum effect.

Clint and Walker stared at each other, and suddenly there was a shotgun blast and the street erupted into gunfire.

Clint wasn't sure what was happening, and apparently neither was Walker. Neither of them had drawn their gun, but everyone else was apparently firing away.

Clint looked beyond Walker and saw Chico Santana go down, then Dog Kelly, whose knives were useless in this situation.

Both Clint and Walker felt that the best they could do was remain still and wait for it to stop raining lead.

Finally, when the shooting died, they looked around and surveyed the damage.

The four hired gunmen were lying in the street, riddled by bullets. Across the street Gimpy Kane was standing over Simon Trehayne, who he had blasted in half with his shotgun.

Clint looked up on the rooftops, and both Jones and Bags waved that they were okay.

The Gunsmith and Gentleman Harry walked over to where Kane was standing.

"What was that about?" Clint asked. "I think the first shot I heard was a shotgun blast."

"It was," Kane said. "This jasper was gonna shoot you while you were concentrating on this man. I didn't have time to do nothing but shoot."

"And your men?" Clint asked Harry.

"They weren't *my* men, but unless Trehayne talked to them behind my back, they didn't know anything about it."

"They went for their guns as soon as Trehayne did, or a split second later," Kane said. "It was like they were watching him, waiting for him to make a move."

"I wouldn't be party to any backshooting, Clint, or to anything along that line."

"I know that, but I guess your friends weren't thinking along the same lines."

"They must have cut their own deal, which suits me fine."

"How do you figure that?"

"I was prepared to do my job, and Trehayne was the one who decided to do it dirty. That released me from my obligation to him or his boss. I can leave town and keep the money. For me to continue on now would make it something personal, and I have nothing personal against you, Clint."

"Nor I against you."

"Adios, then."

"Adios."

"Oh, if you boys are interested," Walker said, as he walked away, "there's eighty grand lying in the street."

Neither Clint nor Kane made a move to pick it up.

"Some street cleaner is really gonna be happy," Kane said.

Back in the sheriff's office Bags and Jones put their rifles down while Kane sat with his shotgun across his lap.

"Well, I'm glad that's over with," Laramie Jones said. "Now we can get out of here."

"I'm sure you've got a bunch of honeys waiting for you over at Jenny Lee's," Kane said.

"And not one of them will touch you without a bath," Clint said.

"That's okay," Jones said. "I always make my women bathe first."

"Well, I guess I'll be going," Clint said.

"Where?" Bags asked.

"Out of town. You don't need me anymore."

"Or us," Kane said, taking off his badge and tossing it on the desk. "Not with your new deputy."

"That reminds me. Hey, Luke?"

Luke Joyner came out from the back, pushing Dallas Tobin ahead of him.

"I told you," Jones said, "all he needed was someone to tell him what to do—the right thing to do."

"Do you think they'll let you deputize him?" Kane asked.

"I don't see why not," Clint answered for Bags. "Bags will just tell the judge how helpful he was."

"That's right," Bags said. "When are you going to leave, Clint?"

"I'm going to leave town first thing tomorrow morning."

"I can't convince you to stay a little longer?"

"No chance," Clint said, shaking his head. "I've had enough excitement for one town."

www.ingramcontent.com/pod-product-compliance
Lightning Source LLC
Chambersburg PA
CBHW020608250626
47154CB00004B/1415